THORNE'S WIFE—the stunning sequel to the unforgettable classic Silhouette Special Edition, THORNE'S WAY. Each book stands alone, and together they're dynamite!

Jonas stared at Valerie in cold fury.

Valerie returned his stare until she thought she'd scream from the tension crackling in the small space that separated them.

When at last he broke the silence, his voice was hard, dismissive, hurtful. "Do whatever the hell you want."

Turning, he stormed from the room, slamming the door behind him with deliberate force.

Val had to bite her lip to stop herself from calling out after him. She took a step forward, then stopped. Not this time, she thought, shaking her head sharply. She would not run after Jonas this time. She had been that route before . . . almost exactly three years before. That time, her impulsive action had inadvertently cost her the life of her unborn child. This time it might cost her the budding life of her individuality.

But he had looked so alone in his fierceness.

Dear Reader,

Once again, six Silhouette **Special Edition** authors present six dramatic new titles aimed at offering you moving, memorable romantic reading. Lindsay McKenna adds another piece to the puzzling, heart-tugging portrait of the noble Trayherns; Joan Hohl revives a classic couple; Linda Shaw weaves a thread of intrigue into a continental affair; Anne Lacey leads us into the "forest primeval"; and Nikki Benjamin probes one man's tortured conscience. Last, but certainly not least, award-winning Karen Keast blends agony and ecstasy into *A Tender Silence*.

What do their books have in common? Each presents men and women you can care about, root for, befriend for life. As Karen Keast puts it:

"What instantly comes to mind when someone mentions *Gone with the Wind*? Rhett and Scarlett. Characterization is the heart of any story; it's what makes you *care* what's happening. In *A Tender Silence*, I strived to portray two people struggling to survive in an imperfect world, a world that doesn't present convenient black-and-white choices. For a writer, the ultimate challenge is to create complex, unique, subtly structured individuals who are, at one and the same time, universally representative."

At Silhouette **Special Edition**, we believe that *people* are at the heart of every satisfying romantic novel, and we hope they find their way into *your* heart. Why not write and let us know?

Best wishes,

Leslie Kazanjian, Senior Editor
Silhouette Books
300 East 42nd Street
New York, N.Y. 10017

JOAN HOHL
Thorne's Wife

Silhouette Special Edition
Published by Silhouette Books New York
America's Publisher of Contemporary Romance

Finally:

Pat Smith and Vivian Stephens;

Nag, nag, nag.

SILHOUETTE BOOKS
300 East 42nd St., New York, N.Y. 10017

ISBN: 0-373-09537-6

First Silhouette Books printing July 1989

Printed in the U.S.A.

Books by Joan Hohl

JOAN HOHL,

a Gemini and an inveterate daydreamer, says she always has her head in the clouds. An avid reader all her life, she discovered romances about ten years ago. "And as soon as I read one," she confesses, "I was hooked." Now an extremely prolific author, she is thrilled to be getting paid for doing exactly what she loves best.

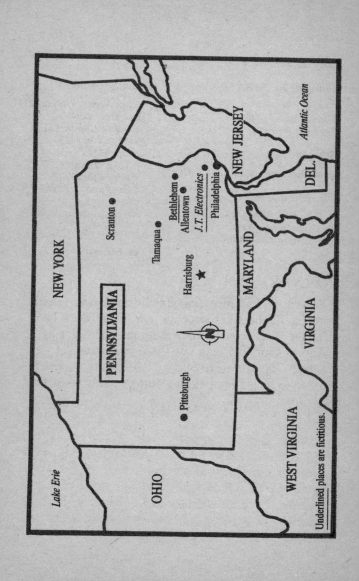

Underlined places are fictitious.

Chapter One

This time I'll kill her!"

The solid thud of the slammed car door punctuated the angry mutter. Settling his long frame behind the steering wheel, Jonas Thorne jabbed the car key into the ignition with an impatient flick of his wrist. The powerful engine under the gleaming black hood of the big Lincoln came to life with a well-tuned purr.

Breathing slowly, deeply, Jonas backed the car out of the space marked for his exclusive use, and with a sweeping movement of one broad hand on the wheel swung the vehicle around on the large lot that surrounded the office complex of J.T. Electronics. Consumed by fury, Jonas didn't spare a glance for the tall building that was the result of his labor. At that moment, every molecule of his body was centered on reaching home and the woman he felt he could happily throttle.

Long months leading into longer years had gone into the making of the taut expression on Jonas's strong, sharply delineated face. Strangely, over the previous three years and until a few hours ago, his face had apparently reversed the aging process, growing younger-looking instead of older. That very morning, one month shy of his forty-second birthday, Jonas had looked younger than he had at thirty-five. Now, ten hours later, he looked every one of his years on earth, and more. For both the young and the old look Jonas had his wife to thank.

His wife. Valerie.

A vision of her captured his imagination and flooded his senses. Valerie—small, delicate and wafer-thin. Valerie—with the elusively haunting beauty of a heart-shaped face, large violet eyes and long, gleaming black hair. Valerie....

Jonas sighed. God! How he loved her!

And, damn! How she infuriated him at times!

Harshly expelling his breath, Jonas drove off the lot and into the flow of early-evening traffic. Handling the car with automatic expertise, he mentally replayed the telephone conversation he'd had earlier that afternoon with Val. His teeth clenched now as they had then.

"Darling," Val had greeted him as always. "I thought I'd better call and tell you not to make any business or social plans that would include me for the week of the twenty-fourth of next month. I'll be in California."

"What?" His mind still assimilating the information in the business report he'd been studying when her call came in, Jonas frowned, positive he'd misunderstood her.

"Jonas, really!" Exasperation was sharp in Val's tone. "Do you ever pay the slightest attention to a word I say?"

"I heard the bit about California." A smile lurked in his deep voice; Val accused him of not listening to her on an average of once a week.

"Yes, Cal-i-for-nia," Val said distinctly.

"Where in California?" he'd asked immediately. "And why, for God's sake?" Jonas had had to strive for the note of indulgence in his voice; Val *had* involved herself in the damnedest projects since the accident that had caused her to miscarry with their child almost three years ago.

Val sighed loudly. "I'm going to attend a rally of the Protect Artistic Individuality group in San Francisco," she'd explained with lessening patience.

Though Jonas snorted at the first part of her reply, he responded to the last in a carefully controlled tone. "San Francisco?" Merely repeating the name of the city evoked the memory of their short honeymoon trip.

"Yes, San Francisco!" Val's tone was edged with suspicion now. "Jonas, are you reading something and talking to me at the same time again?"

Jonas could picture the indignation flushing his wife's lovely face. He grimaced. With a flash of guilt, he acknowledged Val's right to be indignant; he had taken to paying only partial attention whenever she started on the latest of her varied and—at least to him—confusing interests.

"No, Val, I'm not reading."

"You're angry?" Val was never deceived by his even replies. "Again?" she'd snapped.

Up to that point, Jonas had been more confused than angry. Val's barb had further shortened a fuse that had already grown extremely short the past few months. "Forgive me if I'm wrong," he'd retorted sarcastically, "but hadn't we planned to visit San Francisco together?"

There were fully thirty seconds of utter silence before Val exploded. Warned by the lull, Jonas had tilted the receiver away from his ear.

"I absolutely do not believe you have the gall to say that to me, Jonas Thorne! It has been three years...three years!" Val had actually sputtered. "You...you promised to take me back there! Yet not at any time since then have you as much as mentioned returning!" The sound of her erratic breathing came clearly over the connecting wire. "I—I— How dare you say we *planned* to go back together?"

Jonas winced, because every incoherent word was true. "I'll take you in a couple of months," he'd responded, trying to smooth her ruffled feathers.

"I will take myself next month, thank you!" Val slammed her receiver onto the cradle, and Jonas yanked his farther away from his ear.

"Damn it!" he'd growled. "This positively does it!" His own receiver crashed onto the phone console.

Shoving back his desk chair, Jonas had jumped to his feet and marched to the door with every intention of rushing home to straighten out his infuriating wife. He had grasped the door handle, then remembered the meeting he had called with his executives. He had frowned at the slim gold watch on his wrist. He had set up the meeting for four sharp; it was already three minutes after the hour....

Later that afternoon, while adeptly maneuvering the Lincoln from one crowded lane of the bypass to another, Jonas now merely simmered at the memory of his inattention at that meeting. Though he should have been concentrating on new uses of the electrical components under discussion, he'd been reevaluating his marital situation. And with each successive mental step, his frustration had escalated into cold fury. By the time he'd ended the meeting a half hour ago, he had primed himself for a fight.

If only Val had conceived again.

As the still-painful memory of that terrible night unwound in his mind, Jonas's fingers tightened around the leather-covered steering wheel in reaction.

God! What a mess he had made of everything! he recalled, shuddering reflexively. He didn't want to remember that night, yet was powerless to withstand the force of memory's flow.

They had been married two months; two months, during which all hell had seemed to have broken loose, both at home and in the office. Jonas remembered clearly—too clearly—that it had begun the day after the wedding with a phone call from his assistant, Charlie McAndrew.

If he and Valerie had only had some time together, Jonas reflected with a sigh. After the thrilling wedding night they'd shared...if they had only had some private time together. But they had not had that time. Their private time had ended with Charlie's phone call.

Because of a breakthrough Jonas had made in the field of communication systems for space exploration, J.T. Electronics was about to become embroiled in an industry fight with another, failing company, whose president just happened to have friends in very high places in Washington, D.C. The president of this firm had decided to save his floundering company by grabbing a piece of Jonas's action.... But Jonas wasn't about to share his action with anyone.

As he had told Valerie during their rushed return flight from San Francisco to Philadelphia, "No one picks *my* brain."

That had been three years and one month ago. The industrial fight had lasted four weeks but, though Jonas had won the professional battle, he had at the same time apparently lost the personal war. For although their nights together had been sheer heaven for Jonas, he had been too involved with the business battle to devote any of his daytime hours to getting to know his new wife in any way other than physically.

A sharp curl of sensual arousal broke through Jonas's reverie. A wry smile skipped over his thin lips as, savoring the physical discomfort, he noticed that he was almost home. And home, to Jonas, meant Valerie.

Valerie, who had coolly announced that she was going to San Francisco next month without him.

Next month.

June.

Jonas cursed as he remembered the anger and anguish he had lived through three years ago during his birthday month.

Jonas had turned thirty-nine that June. He hadn't cared a damn about that fact. What he had cared about was Valerie's apparent interest in Jean-Paul DeBron, the man his French associate had sent to Jonas as a liaison for the special project they were collaborating on.

The Frenchman had arrived the same day Jonas's daughter, Mary Beth, came home from the finishing school she had been attending in Switzerland. Lynn, Jonas's ex-wife, had returned to the States with her daughter. Marge, Jonas's beloved ex-mother-in-law, rounded out the group.

Even now, three years later, the memory of that day retained enough power to wrench a groan from Jonas. The entire day had proved to be a debacle. In retrospect, Jonas accepted the guilt not only for ruining his daughter's homecoming, but for having put his new bride at such a disadvantage.

Jealousy. Damn, Jonas hated the word. But what was more important, he hated what the emotion had done to him three years ago. His long fingers gripped the steering wheel so tightly that the skin paled over his broad knuckles. Grimacing, he forced himself to relax his grip.

The memory ate at his mind like acid.

If he hadn't been so damned jealous and so scared of losing Val, he wouldn't have been blind to the brother-sister affection between Val and Jean-Paul, or to the growing love between the Frenchman and his daughter.

But Jonas had been blinded by his own unreasonable jealousy to the extent that, when Val told him she was pregnant, he had actually accused her of being unfaithful.

The big car was air-conditioned, yet Jonas's brow was beaded with perspiration. Cursing beneath his breath, he carefully monitored his driving, while reliving the horror of the consequences of his accusation.

Knowing he was wrong to accuse her, Jonas had apologized almost at once, then had turned and left the house. Valerie had run after him. As he backed around in the driveway, Jonas hadn't seen her running toward his car. He could still hear the echo of his own cry of warning on catching her fleeting image in the rearview mirror. But his warning came too late. The back end of his car struck her a glancing blow, and Valerie had suffered a miscarriage later that night.

Jonas knew that he would go to his grave blaming himself for the accident.

Valerie wanted a child so very badly. How very different their life together would be today, if only she had conceived again.

Like Val, Jonas longed for a child from their union. He wanted a son.... Hadn't his desire for a son been the reason for proposing marriage to Val in the first place?

Oh, sure Thorne, you bet. The jeering voice of his conscience mocked Jonas. Desire had first, last and always been the reason for his proposal.

Recalling that far from romantic proposal, Jonas's lips tilted derisively. At the time he had in actual fact offered Val a business proposition. In exchange for his name, wealth and protection, all Val had to do was give him a son. Yet from the outset, Jonas had known full well that he had acted on the strength of the attraction he felt for her. Val, then his personal secretary, was simply playing havoc with his libido by showing up for work every day.

The jarring blare of a car horn, too close for comfort, jolted Jonas back into the present. If he wasn't careful, he advised himself scathingly, he wouldn't *live* to challenge Val's decision to go to California without him.

His thoughts centered once more on making it home in one piece, Jonas concentrated anew on the traffic weaving in and out and around him until he turned the car onto the private lane that ended in a circular driveway before the house he had had built over two years ago.

Pulling the Lincoln to a stop in front of the four-car garage, Jonas stepped out and slammed the door behind him. Anger simmering at near boiling point, he strode along the flagstone path to the front door of the trilevel glass and redwood house. Key at the ready, he shoved it into the lock, only to curse fluently when the door opened with the turn of the knob.

How many times had he cautioned Val about keeping the door locked when he wasn't at home? Jonas railed inwardly, marching into the house. And *she* had the temerity to accuse *him* of never paying attention!

Jonas paused in the black and white marble foyer, his nostrils flaring as he sniffed the air. Val was doing her thing again in the kitchen, he decided, noting the

delicate aroma of cooking food. What was it this
time? he mused. Stir-fry? Greek? Tex-Mex? Closing
his eyes, he inhaled deeply and identified the mouth-
watering scent of shrimp tempura.

The low rumble of Jonas's stomach reminded him
that he'd forgotten to eat lunch—as usual. Moving
with his normal long-legged, loose-limbed gait along
the hallway to the kitchen, his eyes narrowed with
suspicion.

Valerie knew how much he enjoyed her stir-fried
meals. Had she hoped to avoid a confrontation by
preparing his favorite rice and shrimp tempura dish?
If that had been her plan, Jonas thought unmollified,
Valerie Thorne was in for an unpleasant surprise.

But as he drew nearer to the kitchen, Jonas's appetite sharpened with the increasing strength of the tantalizing aroma. Damn! He was hungry, he grumbled
to himself. Maybe he'd wait until after dinner to
throttle her.

Pausing in the kitchen archway, Jonas propped one
shoulder against the smooth wall and ran his narrow-
eyed gaze over the small, slender form of his wife. She
was standing at the stove, her back to him, humming
softly as she busied herself with two long-handled
utensils.

From the back, Valerie looked more like a teenager
than a mature, thirty-one-year-old woman. A frothy,
lace-trimmed apron was tied in a large bow at the back
of her tiny waist, protecting her paisley cotton skirt.
A leaf-green sleeveless blouse was neatly tucked into
the waistband of the skirt. Slim-heeled sandals com-
plemented her small, narrow feet. Her glorious mane
of gleaming black hair was piled into a haphazard
mass on top of her head, revealing her slender neck.

Jonas's teeth ached with a sudden overwhelming need to nip at her satiny skin. Compressing his lips, he swallowed a groan. The mere sight of her, even her back, aroused an appetite much sharper than the one tormenting his stomach. The hunger for food could easily be appeased by regular meals or even periodic snacks. Yet oddly, the hunger Jonas felt for Val had never truly been slaked, no matter how many times he availed himself of her ardently offered bounty. If anything, each and every physical encounter with Val left Jonas hungry for more. It had been that way between them from their very first time together on their wedding night.

Feeling himself beginning to weaken, Jonas straightened and squared his broad shoulders, reminding himself that this time Val had gone too far.

"You are *not* going to San Francisco next month, and that's final." Although his voice was low, it held steely conviction. If Jonas hoped to get the advantage by startling Val—and he had—he succeeded admirably.

Emitting a tiny screech, Val whipped around to face him. "Darn you, Jonas!" she exclaimed. "How dare you sneak up on me like that?" Still clutching her tools, Val planted her fists on her hips and glared at him. "Are you trying to give me heart failure?" she demanded, her eyes flashing angry warning signals.

"And rob myself of the pleasure of beating you?" Jonas retorted, arrogantly raising one ash-brown eyebrow.

Valerie mirrored his expression with a perfectly arched black brow. "You wouldn't dare," she taunted confidently.

"Don't make book on it, sweetheart." Jonas sauntered into the room as he offered the advice. "There is a limit to how much I'll put up with from you."

Valerie angled her chin defiantly. "Oh, heavens, please don't frighten me like this." She didn't sound frightened; she didn't look intimidated, either. "I'm going to California, Jonas, and there's nothing you can do about it." Casually turning her back on him, she attacked the large wok once more. "Dinner will be ready in a few minutes." Beginning to hum again, she gently stirred the shrimp.

"Damn it, Val!" Frustrated, Jonas grasped her by one arm and swung her around to face him, feigning retreat as one utensil flashed by his head.

"How would you like to be skewered?" Val brandished the two-pronged fork threateningly.

"How would you like to be—?"

"Jonas!" Val's sharp exclamation covered his words. "Don't be crude," she admonished, lips twitching with her attempt to contain a smile. "At least not before dinner."

Jonas wanted to maintain his anger.... An errant smile of his own defeated him. "I really should beat you, you know," he muttered. "But I won't." His tone thickened to the consistency of honey. "At least not before dinner."

"How magnanimous of you," Val drawled.

"Yeah, I know," Jonas retorted. Bending swiftly, he gave her a quick, hard kiss, then swung away before she could raise her culinary weapon. At the kitchen archway, he paused again to shoot a glance at her, a blatantly sexy smile curving his lips now. "On second thought, I don't believe I will beat you," he said slowly in a low, enticing tone. "I have other, in-

finitely more effective methods to change your mind."
Whistling softly, he ambled from the room.

And those methods usually work too, darn it! Val
acknowledged in silence as she returned her attention
to her meal. While she stirred the contents of the wok,
she absently skimmed the tip of her tongue over her
lips, savoring the taste that was uniquely Jonas. Feeling desire uncurl deep inside her, Val sighed and shook
herself free of the web of sensuality he had so effort-
lessly woven around her.

Not this time, she promised herself grimly. She was
going to San Francisco, and nothing Jonas could say
or do would dissuade her. Not because she was all that
fervently dedicated to the cause of preserving artistic
individuality. The individuality Val was dedicated to
preserving was her own. Jonas's personality was so
very strong that Val actively feared she'd be swallowed up by it if she didn't assert herself. San Francisco was Val's statement on the subject.

Dashing into the powder room off the front foyer,
Val checked her makeup while removing the large
butterfly hair clips that anchored her black mane. A
quick attack with a brush, a shrug of her shoulders,
and she was dashing back into the kitchen, her sharp-
eyed gaze sweeping the table as she passed the archway that led into the dining room.

The oval cherry wood table was set for two with
delicate china, lead crystal and sterling silver cutlery
on wide, lacy place mats. An arrangement of spring
blossoms with two tall slim candles rising from their
midst stood in the center of the table.

Val was removing two wooden bowls of salad from
the crisper drawer in the refrigerator when she caught
sight of Jonas's tall figure entering the kitchen. He had

removed his suit jacket and necktie, had opened the two top buttons of his pale blue shirt and had rolled up the sleeves, revealing his lightly haired forearms. The sight of him, so tall, muscularly slender and devastatingly handsome in his chiseled, rugged way, caused a tremor in Val's arms. The bowls tilted precariously, nearly dumping the salad onto the floor. With a sigh of acceptance, Val concentrated on steadying both her hands and the contents of the bowls.

It was always the same, Val mused, backing away from the fridge. Even after three years of marriage and the difficulties they had been through, Jonas didn't have to do anything but walk into a room to set her pulse racing.

"Is there something I can do to help?" he asked, offering assistance, as he never failed to do. Val had adamantly refused to hire a housekeeper.

"Yes." Val shut the fridge door with a sideways nudge of her hip. "You can take these in to the table." She handed him the bowls. "Oh, and light the candles, please," she called after him.

"What about wine?" Jonas asked a moment later from the dining-room archway, where he stood watching her transfer the food from the wok to serving dishes.

"You choose." Glancing up, Val frowned at the smile that was tugging at his sculpted mouth. She knew absolutely nothing about wine, which never failed to amuse Jonas. Sweeping by him with the large serving tray, Val promised herself that someday she'd enroll for a course on wine appreciation—if and when she ever found the time.

Jonas knew quite a lot about wine, and the one he chose had just the proper texture to complement their meal.

Sipping the pale gold liquid from the fragile flute, Val watched Jonas as he eagerly consumed three-quarters of the food she'd placed on the table. Meanwhile, she merely made a show of eating the small portion she'd taken.

After long months of hard work, Val had finally achieved her goal of getting into a size three dress again. She was almost frantic in her determination to maintain that size—and the weight of ninety-six pounds that she had not seen registered on the scales since before meeting Jonas.

On the other hand, Jonas seemed equally determined to see her eat her way back to the size six she'd attained after losing their baby. This evening, other than making the occasional pointed remark, he said nothing about her meager intake. But when she served a single dessert—his—he scowled in a familiar way that warned Val of an approaching argument.

"No dessert?" Jonas arched his brows into an exaggerated peak.

Val's sigh spoke of long endurance of this boring topic. "Jonas, I have not been eating desserts for months now." Her expression was a study in controlled patience. "One really does not require dessert to survive." Smiling serenely, she sipped at her wine. Her smile was a goad to his temper, and she knew it. Pondering on the urge that drove her to continually challenge him, she calmly observed the storm brewing in his gray-blue eyes.

"No, one doesn't need dessert to survive," Jonas agreed, returning her smile in a way that shot a thrill composed of equal parts of apprehension and excitement through Valerie. "But one might have to be very careful when speaking to one's husband. Do you get my drift?" he asked quietly—too quietly.

"Why, Mr. Thorne, sir!" Val fluttered her eyelashes flirtatiously. "Are you threatening little ol' me?" Her attempt at a Southern accent was appallingly bad—deliberately.

Jonas was not amused. "Keep pushing, sweetheart," he warned, an edge of annoyance in his tone now.

"And then what?" Val taunted, asking herself why she persisted when he was obviously becoming angry all over again. Of course, she knew full well why; she was damn tired of being treated like a second-class person—in other words like a wife!

"I'll be left with two choices," Jonas informed her smoothly. "I'll either have to ignore you," he said, "or make very rough love to you, which I'd enjoy immensely." His shrug was eloquent.

"Promises, promises," Val chanted, suddenly breathless and commending herself on the evenness of her tone. Sliding her chair away from the table, she rose with unstudied grace. Taking advantage of the opportunity to look down on the man who stood a good foot taller than she did, Val couldn't resist one last shot. "You're all talk and little action, Thorne." Scooping up the tray of now empty dishes, she beat a hasty retreat into the kitchen.

Valerie expected Jonas to stalk after her—and he did. Her excitement churning to near fever pitch, she shot a glance at the wall clock. A sigh that was a mixture of relief and disappointment whispered through her lips when the door chimes pealed, just as Jonas was reaching for her.

"Now who in hell . . . ?" he began in a low growl.

"Oh! Did I forget to tell you?" Val managed a helpless look of confusion. "I expect it's your daughter and son-in-law." Swinging away from him, she smiled sweetly. "Mary Beth called earlier to ask if we'd mind if she and Jean-Paul stopped by tonight. She said they have something to tell us." She paused in the hallway to give him an arched glance. "Since I thought I might need their protection, I told them we wouldn't mind at all." Val grinned at the muttered curse that followed her to the front door.

Before Val set foot on the marble floor in the foyer, Jonas was by her side. "Having fun, are you?" he growled, striding past her to the door. "Make the most of it, my love," he murmured. As his hand grasped the brass latch, his glittering gaze swept her figure. "Mary Beth and Jean-Paul will have to go home sometime." Not giving her time to respond, he pulled open the door.

"Hi, Dad." Mary Beth stepped into the foyer, grinning as if she'd just won the lottery. At twenty-three, Mary Beth was a lovely young woman. Tall and clear-featured like her father and golden-skinned like her mother, she had a look uniquely her own with her soft eyes and mouth and honey-blond hair . . . which was several shades darker than Jonas's ash blond. "I hope you don't mind us dropping in on the spur of the moment like this?'' she asked, grinning impishly.

"Not at all," Jonas assured her with what Val considered commendable aplomb for a man on the verge of going up in smoke. "We had no plans for this evening." Reaching out, he accepted the hand his son-in-law offered—thinking it slightly comical, considering he'd left Jean-Paul in the conference room at J.T. Electronics less than two hours ago. "Jean-Paul," he drawled, quietly shutting the door.

"Jonas." The handsome Frenchman smiled in appreciation of the irony in the formality of the handshake.

"Jean-Paul, will you look at the figure on this woman!" Mary Beth exclaimed dramatically, motioning toward Valerie. "What are you living on, Val, cottage cheese and low cal air?"

"Just about," Jonas muttered as he led the way into the spacious living room.

"Oh, Jonas, really!" Val protested, frowning at his expression of disapproval.

Coming up beside her, Jean-Paul slipped an arm around Val's tiny waist. "You look *magnifique, ma petite*," he said, brushing her soft cheek with his lips. "Quite like the young woman I met in France over four years ago."

Val smiled gratefully and returned his kiss. "*Merci*, Jean-Paul."

"And I feel like a cow in comparison!" Mary Beth wailed, running her palms over her own slender curves.

Jean-Paul sent her a smoldering look. "If you would care to return home, my sweet, I would be delighted to demonstrate how very much I adore little blond cows."

Laughing softly, Val gave Jean-Paul a quick, fierce hug; she would always love Jean-Paul, who had come within two weeks of being her brother-in-law, love him in a very special way. And it was obvious to everyone who knew them that Jean-Paul returned her affection.

Hands on hips, Mary Beth glared at her husband before rolling her beautiful blue eyes at Valerie. "I swear, Val, do men ever think of *anything* other than bedroom games?"

"Your father does," Val replied, sliding a glance at Jonas. "He thinks mainly about electrical components and computers and such." Moving easily but purposefully, she headed for the hallway and escape. "Now if you'll excuse me, I must finish clearing the dinner table."

The laughter that erupted from Mary Beth and Jean-Paul didn't drown the ominous tone of Jonas's voice.

"Valerie, come back here."

"In a few minutes." She called the response over her shoulder from her relatively safe position in the hall. "I'll bring a tray of coffee with me." Smiling to herself, Val returned to the dining room and the dishes cluttering the table.

Mary Beth joined her in the kitchen as she was stacking the dishes in the dishwasher. "Can I help with anything?"

Val smiled at her stepdaughter, who was only seven years her junior. "Yes. You can start the coffee if you like." She raised her eyebrows. "Don't tell me, let me guess. Your father and Jean-Paul are talking business?"

"What else?" Mary Beth shrugged. As she ran water into the glass coffeepot, she slanted a contemplative glance at Valerie. "Are you and Dad having problems, Val?"

"Problems?" Val repeated, frowning as she switched on the machine before turning to look at the younger woman. "What do you mean?"

"Oh, come on, Val!" Mary Beth grimaced. "Don't pull that blank confusion act with me. I thought . . . believed . . . we were friends."

"We are!" Val exclaimed. "But—"

"But nothing!" Mary Beth interrupted. "I've been married long enough to read the signals, and both you and Dad are sending them out. Good grief! You two have been taking verbal potshots at each other for months now. I don't want to pry, really, but I'm concerned. Jean-Paul's concerned, too."

Val felt trapped. What could she say? She and Jonas were having problems, personality problems, but she certainly wasn't about to confide in his daughter—regardless of how fond of the young woman she'd become.

"I suspect all married couples have their off moments," Val replied vaguely. "Your father and I are no different than most." Avoiding Mary Beth's skeptical look, she turned to the kitchen cabinet to remove cups and saucers.

"There...ah..." Mary Beth hesitated. "There isn't another woman involved.... Is there, Val?"

The fragile china rattled in Valerie's hands as she spun to face a frowning Mary Beth. "Another woman?" Sheer amazement raised her natural soft tone several decibels. "No!" she exclaimed. "Of course there's no other woman! Why would you even think—?"

"I don't!" Mary Beth interjected forcefully. "Not really. It's just...well..." Her shoulders lifted and fell in a helpless movement. "Suddenly you and Dad seem to be drifting apart, and I was afraid that..." Her voice trailed away on a sigh.

So it was beginning to show. Hiding her thoughts, Val busied her hands by arranging the china on a tray. How many others had noticed the strain between Jonas and herself? Val wondered tiredly. And how long would it be before she found herself in the position of fielding polite inquiries from other curious, well-meaning friends? She stifled a groan. The prospect was daunting. Giving up the pretense of busywork, she raised her eyes to meet Mary Beth's concerned gaze.

"There is no other woman, Mary Beth." Solid conviction underlined Val's tone, conviction instilled by her absolute trust in Jonas. While it was true that they were having some marital trouble, Val was positive the problems weren't of the *other woman* variety.

Mary Beth was visibly relieved. "I'm glad. You've been so very good for Dad, Val," she said earnestly.

She had? A startled laugh burst from Val. "Do you really think so?" Privately she had doubts—many, many doubts.

"Yes, of course." Mary Beth's response was flatteringly prompt. "All I have to do is look at him. Dad looks five years younger than he did five years ago."

Val's violet eyes darkened with memory. "Your father was always a dynamic, attractive man." Her voice had softened.

"And he is even more dynamic and attractive than before." Mary Beth grinned. "He smiles more, and Dad always did have one fantastic smile."

"I'll say!" Val exclaimed. For an instant she felt again the heady, stunned reaction she'd experienced the very first time she saw Jonas smile; and he'd smiled at another woman on that occasion! "I couldn't begin to explain the effect his first smile had on me."

"Like being poleaxed?" Mary Beth teased.

Val pretended to consider. "That comes pretty close," she agreed, grinning when the younger girl giggled. "It also comes pretty close to what he'll do to us," she went on brusquely, "if we don't get this coffee in to him." Reaching around the grinning Mary Beth, Val drew a white coffee thermos from the countertop. "I'll pour the coffee into this. You can get the cream and sugar."

"What, no cake or cookies?" Mary Beth's brows arched. "Dad loves desserts."

"And he's had his." A smile eased Val's adamant tone. "I'm watching his weight for him."

Mary Beth was still smiling when she carried the tray into the living room. As her husband leaped from his chair to take the tray from her, her father challenged her smile.

"I know that particular smirk, kid." Jonas's tone smacked of parental indulgence. "What have you and Val been up to?"

Mary Beth burst out laughing. "Not dessert, that's for sure. Val assures me that *she*'s watching *your* weight."

"Val would do better to provide the dessert," Jonas retorted. "And then eat it herself." He raked his wife's ultraslim figure with a hard-eyed glance. "If she gets much thinner," he added, "I'll have to tether her to something, to prevent her from blowing away with the slightest breeze."

"But, Jonas! I think Valerie looks wonderful." Jean-Paul ran an appreciative look over her. "She looks exactly as she did when I first met her."

Jonas shifted his narrowed gaze to his son-in-law. "So you said before," he replied evenly. "Personally, I prefer her the way she looked when *I* first met her."

Yes; overweight, undernourished, scared and submissive. Val prudently kept the response to herself, but felt positive that this attitude of his lay behind their inability to communicate. Jonas insisted on casting her in the role of *his* wife, *his* hostess, *his* ornament, and altogether submissive—whereas she was determined to become *her* own person.

Raising her cup to her lips, Val sighed into the dark brew. It had been an uphill battle all the way and, as the remark Jonas had just made proved, she wasn't even near the top of her particular goal-mountain.

Evidently not in the least put off by Jonas's cool attitude, Jean-Paul shrugged in the way only a Frenchman can. "Then we shall have to agree to disagree, eh?" His teeth were a flash of white against his dark skin.

Jonas didn't smile. "If we must."

"Oh, for the sake of harmony, I think we must." Jean-Paul's eyes crinkled with inner amusement as he shot a sparkling glance at his wife.

Jonas was alert at once. Shifting his sharp gaze from Mary Beth to Jean-Paul, then to Val, he slowly replaced his cup on its matching saucer. "What's going on?" he demanded of Val.

Since she was asking herself the same question, Val shrugged. "I haven't the vaguest idea." Her eyes moved in unison with his to the couple seated side by side on the long sofa.

"Well?" Jonas prompted, when it appeared that all the two were capable of was smiling smugly.

Their smiles widening still more, Mary Beth and Jean-Paul glanced at each other, then back to Val and Jonas—who by this time was showing distinct signs of thinning patience. Then they rushed into speech simultaneously.

"I'm pregnant!"

"We're going to have a child."

There was an instant of utter silence, then Val and Jonas responded in unison.

"How wonderful for you both!" Val exclaimed.

"Honey, I'm delighted for you." Springing from his chair, Jonas crossed to the sofa, pulled up Mary Beth and gathered her into his arms, while extending his right hand to Jean-Paul. "I'm delighted for you, too," he added with a grin.

Following at her husband's heels, Val took her turn at bestowing excited hugs on the glowing pair. Then her eyes flashed at Jonas as Mary Beth stated what would soon be obvious to everyone.

"You're going to be a grandfather, Dad!"

Chapter Two

A *grandfather*. He was going to be a grandfather.

His mouth curved in a wry smile, Jonas turned off the shower spray and stepped out of the ceramic tile stall. His Mary Beth, his baby, was going to have a baby.

Suddenly tired, Jonas muffled a yawn with one hand, reaching with the other for a brown-and-white-striped oversize towel that was neatly folded over a long gleaming chrome rack mounted on the wall.

Though he seldom retired much before midnight, tonight it was even later than usual. It had been after one before Mary Beth and Jean-Paul departed for home, thanks to the impromptu celebration they'd put on—complete with a snack Val and Mary Beth had

prepared and the bottle of imported champagne Jonas
had provided for the occasion.

Where had all the years gone? Jonas mused, drying
his body with absentminded sweeps of the thick bath
sheet. By his reckoning, Mary Beth still seemed little
more than a baby herself. And yet in seven months or
so his little girl, his baby, would make him a grandfather.

Jonas couldn't decide whether he liked the idea or
not. It wasn't so much the fact of being a grandfather
as the word's connotations of age. Though there were
days when Jonas felt a hundred and twelve, usually he
didn't yet feel old enough to be a grandfather.

His Mary Beth. Picturing the sweet-natured, gold-
en-haired little girl who had run into his arms whenever he'd managed to make it home from the office
before her bedtime, Jonas sighed. His baby. Feeling
the pressure of time, he glanced into the full-length
mirror on the door.

Was he getting old? He'd be forty-two next month.
Was forty-two old? His lids narrowed over his gray-
blue eyes, Jonas studied his reflection, searching for
telltale signs of encroaching age. He didn't have to
look very hard. The sprinkling of gray that had merely
peppered the thick, abundant ash-blond hair at his
temples a few years ago had grown into wings of solid
silver. The lines radiating from his eyes and bracket-
ing his mouth had deepened into permanent grooves.
His brow was creased. He acknowledged with a vague
sense of dissatisfaction that all these signs were definite indications of middle age.

On the other hand, his face and form still retained vestiges of youth and vigor, Jonas decided with wry humor, as he scanned his reflected image.

There was a sheen of health in the skin that stretched tautly over his big-boned, sharply defined facial features. His eyes were clear, shrewd, intelligent. His tall form still had the flat, angular look of youth, the musculature long and steel-hard rather than bunched and flabby. His hips and waist were still narrow, his belly flat to slightly concave.

Turning away from his reflection, Jonas tossed the towel into the clothes hamper and shrugged into the black silk robe Val had given him the previous Christmas. Recalling his initial reaction to the gift, Jonas smiled with self-mockery.

Jonas had never considered himself a robe type; he was either dressed or undressed. That being the case, he knew his expression had been one of consternation when he opened the elaborately wrapped package on Christmas morning. Not wanting to hurt Val, he'd infused a note of enthusiasm into his voice as he thanked her for the present.

Proving she knew him better than he had suspected, Val had laughed and said, "I know you're thinking that it's too sybaritic for you."

She was correct.

Jonas had concurred with a grunted, "Damn right."

"But you're wrong," Val had continued, ignoring his mutter of agreement. "I knew it was for you the moment I saw it." Leaning over him, she had curled her arms around his neck and nibbled delicately on his earlobe. "Please, darling, try it on for me. I just know you're going to look as sexy as the devil in it."

Since it was very early on Christmas morning, hours before Mary Beth, Jean-Paul and Marge were due to arrive for the traditional meal and exchange of gifts, Jonas and Val had been sitting on their huge bed to exchange their personal gifts.

"Sexy, hmm?" Though Jonas had laughed, he had modeled the robe for her—after a mutually exciting interlude—and had worn it nearly every evening since then.

Feeling the silk glide against his skin brought back the fiery excitement of that holiday morning. Desire, hot and swift, flared through Jonas, burning away his sleepiness, searing his tired body into taut revival. Suddenly needing the sensations only Val could arouse in him, he raked a brush through his hair and pulled open the bathroom door.

Maybe he wasn't quite as old as he had almost convinced himself he was.

The sight that met his eyes as he walked into the bedroom drew from him a sigh made up of equal parts of amusement and frustration.

Her only covering a minuscule scrap of white satin panties, Val was on the floor in a hatha-yoga shoulder stand. Her slim body rose into the air, straight as an arrow from the base of her neck and the edge of her shoulders. Her arms lay relaxed and limp on the carpet. Her eyes were closed. Her breathing was measured, even and regular. Her small, rose-tipped breasts shivered with each breath.

Jonas had become so accustomed to observing Val in a variety of exercise positions that he was no longer fazed. Yet, seeing her this time in that particular upside-down position for some inexplicable reason added fuel to the fire raging in his body.

Obeying an impulse, Jonas padded toward her across the lush carpet. Halting mere inches from her raised legs, he reached out and stroked his broad hands over her slender, shapely calves. Fire licked through his veins when he felt her muscles quiver in reaction and heard the catch in her breathing pattern.

"Jonas." Val didn't open her eyes as she murmured his name in a tone of admonition.

Ignoring the warning, Jonas curled his long fingers around her ankles. Gently applying pressure, he drew down her body until her weight was resting on the upper part of her back. Then, parting her legs, he stepped forward and tucked them neatly around his waist.

Val's eyes flew open. "Jonas! What are you—? Oh!" She gasped aloud as he slid one palm down the inside of her thigh. "What are you thinking of?"

"I'm thinking that this position you're in has very definite possibilities," Jonas murmured, stroking the underside of her knees with his fingertips.

So delicately balanced, Val couldn't move. Jonas knew she couldn't move. She knew that he knew she couldn't move. His smile was slow, sexy and incredibly exciting. Val shivered with anticipation.

Jonas didn't disappoint her. Savoring the tightness coiling inside him, he let his hand drift with excruciating slowness to the satin barrier at the apex of her thighs.

Valerie didn't disappoint *him*. Murmuring low in her throat, she moved her body against his tingling palm. Jonas shuddered in reaction to the sensation that streaked like lightning from his hand to every nerve ending in his body. The intensity of the desire clamoring inside him was slightly shocking... considering that they had slept side by side for three years.

Would he never get enough of her? Jonas asked himself, responding to her sensuous movements by stroking his long fingers over the heated satin beneath his hand.

The query was the last cohesive thought to form in Jonas's head for some time. Moaning his name, Valerie moved against him in invitation. Her action cleared his mind of all considerations except the overpowering need that was storming his senses and converging on the center of his masculinity.

Forgetting the comfort of the enormous bed behind him, Jonas continued to stroke her through the warm satin while he slowly sank to his knees. Within seconds both his robe and the scrap of fabric swathing Valerie's hips lay in a shimmering heap on the carpet beside him.

Old? Middle-aged? Ha!

Silent laughter rippled through Jonas as he slid his taut aroused body between her silky thighs. The encroaching years were meaningless, powerless against the surge of vigor now quickening his body. Valerie and his unquenchable hunger for her kept him young, vital . . . hot.

Sliding his hands beneath her, Jonas held Val's undulating hips still. Denying the urgency shuddering through him, he entered her slowly, savoring the thrill of burying the strongest and most vulnerable part of himself deeply within the velvet softness of her body. Excitement took a quantum leap inside him when Val grasped his thighs and sank her nails reflexively into his quivering muscles.

"Jonas." Valerie's husky whisper contained both a plea and a command.

He granted both. Bending to her, Jonas captured her mouth with his in a hard, hungry kiss. Then, spurred by her throaty murmurs, he speared his tongue into the depths of her sweetness, initiating a rhythm of complete possession that was reflected by the movement of his body. Impelled by a need beyond his comprehension, Jonas drove his body relentlessly toward the goal of utter ecstasy. Gritting his teeth, he denied himself until he felt the first of the cascading shudders that began pulsating through Val. Then, releasing his restraint, Jonas made the final thrust, crying her name in a hoarse groan as he was swept into the vortex with her.

Valerie couldn't breathe. She couldn't think. She could only feel. Her entire body sensitized, she gloried in the tension coiling ever tighter inside with each stroke and thrust of Jonas's hard body. Quivering, she abandoned herself to sensation. It was always the same, yet ever different. Clutching his taut flanks, Val strained to draw him deeper within herself, at that instant needing the fullness of him more than she needed breath to survive.

Forgotten was the discord between them. There had never been discord while they were locked together, united in the most intimate embrace of lovers. And Valerie loved Jonas with every part of her being. The clawing need robbing her of thought and inhibition was a direct response to the depth of the love she felt for him. In three years, Valerie had never had enough of his lovemaking, and never felt completely satiated. She always craved more, more, and still more of Jonas.

Valerie made a strangled sound of surprised pleasure when release caught her, and gasped in appreciation of his final driving thrust. Fusing together, clinging to each other, they rode the wave of completion.

"You know I love you." Jonas's voice was ragged from his uneven breathing.

"Yes." Val smiled. Jonas never spoke the words of love while performing the act of love. He always waited until they had attained the heights of passion before speaking aloud his innermost feelings, complimenting her with his declaration after sharing his pleasure with her. "As you know I love you," she murmured, returning the compliment.

"Do you?" Levering his body away from her, Jonas stared into her eyes as he stretched his length on the carpet beside her.

"Jonas!" Val didn't try to conceal the confusion and hurt his question caused her. "You know I do."

"Then why in hell are you going to San Francisco without me?" Jonas demanded, ruthlessly searching her shadowed violet eyes.

The discord between them was back, weighing Val down with disappointment and depression. She escaped his piercing stare by closing her eyes. "I've explained why I'm going," she answered in a weary tone. "I'm going in support of the—"

Jonas cut her off impatiently. "I don't believe you."

Was she so very transparent? Val asked herself, trembling in reaction to the harshness of his tone. Could Jonas see through her so easily? Did he know, understand or even care that she was fighting an uphill battle to move out of the shade of his protective, smothering shadow and establish her own identity? Didn't he realize that she couldn't be a true mate or partner to him until she became all she could be as a woman?

Anger dried the tears gathering in Valerie's eyes. Opening them, she gave him a glittering look. "Are you calling me a liar, Jonas?"

"No." His denial held conviction.

"But you just said that you don't believe me," she reminded him pointedly.

"I don't believe that you're that concerned with protecting artistic individuality." As usual, Jonas swore when he was mad. "Damn it, Val, you've been involving yourself in one pursuit after another for months." His eyes narrowed; his harsh voice lashed at her once more. "Are you bored with this marriage?" He paused, then added in a dangerously soft tone, "Or are you bored with me?"

"Bored?" Her expression incredulous, Val jerked into a sitting position. "You can ask me that after what just happened here?" She indicated their carpet-bed with a sweep of her small hand.

Obviously uncomfortable with having her glare down at him, Jonas sprang up beside her. "Well, damn it, Val, you must be dissatisfied with something," he insisted, grinding out the words.

"For your information, dissatisfied is not synonymous with bored," Val said, scrambling to her feet so that she could look down at him again, even while admitting to herself that her action was childish.

As if not to be bested, and revealing a streak of immaturity himself, Jonas rose to tower over her. "Then you admit to being dissatisfied?" Accusation colored his tone; a ruddy hue tinged his prominent cheekbones.

Tamping down an urge to climb onto the bed to gain additional height, Valerie tilted her chin defiantly and glared up into his stormy steel-blue eyes. "Yes," she said distinctly. "I am dissatisfied."

Her boldness seemed to stop him cold for an instant. Then, his movement calculated, Jonas turned to rake a gaze over the carpet. "You didn't appear to be dissatisfied a few minutes ago," he said as he returned his gaze to hers. "Or was your response an act, put on to appease me?" His eyes were the icy color of the Atlantic Ocean in the dead of winter.

Valerie might have shivered in the face of his cold stare, if it hadn't been for the flash of hot fury that seared through her. Angrier with him than she had ever been, she reacted to his accusation without thought or consideration or even instinctive self-preservation. Val's arm flew up and out. Her palm connected with his cheek with a stinging, resounding whack. Valerie felt the rippling force of the blow from her palm to her shoulder and all the way down to the base of her spine.

"How dare you accuse me of putting on that kind of act?" she cried, snatching her burning palm away from his face. A sinking sensation invaded her stomach as she watched a fiery imprint of her palm form on his pale skin.

Jonas had gone deathly still, for long moments not even appearing to breathe. The only living things about him were his eyes, and the expression in them nearly scared the life out of Valerie. In their sea-tossed depths she could see the inner battle he was fighting against the need to lash out and strike back at her.

Until that moment, Val had never felt an instant of physical fear of Jonas. Now, fear crawled through her veins like a cold-blooded viper. If Jonas lost his inner battle and struck her, she would go down like a felled tree, and she knew it. What was more, Val also knew she'd deserve it.

But she wouldn't run. She couldn't run! She could barely breathe.... Her spine rigid, Val endured his chilling stare, awaiting the outcome. The breath eased from her constricted chest a heartbeat after Jonas exhaled harshly.

"That was a close call, Valerie." His voice was tight with strain.

Relief brought a sheen of tears to her eyes. "I'm sorry, Jonas," she whispered.

"Don't ever dare to hit me again."

Val bristled. "And don't you ever again dare to accuse me of putting on an act to appease you."

Jonas had the grace to back down. "I'm sorry for that. I knew it wasn't true when I said it."

"I shouldn't have allowed it to hurt me." She sighed. "You've accused me unjustly before." Val was immediately sorry for the indictment.

Jonas winced, revealing the pain he had refused to acknowledge from her physical blow. His eyes grew dark, betraying the unceasing inner torment. With her unbridled tongue, she had sliced through the fabric of their past three years together, exposing the wound still open and bleeding in his soul. He *had* accused her unjustly before, knowing while he did so that it wasn't true. In consequence, an accident had caused Val to miscarry with their child. Jonas was still paying the price.

"Jonas." Hurting for him, Val reached out to him. It was when her palm touched his warm bare skin that she remembered that they were both still naked. It didn't matter. In comparison to the exposure of lingering pain in the soul, naked skin was of little importance. With a mental shrug, she stepped forward to slide her arms around his waist. Tears running freely down her face, she held him close, offering compassion and comfort, gratefully accepting the same from him when Jonas enclosed her within his crushing embrace.

"I'm sorry, Val." His voice was low and unsteady, and Valerie knew he was apologizing for his past as well as his present unfounded accusations.

"It's all right, Jonas." Val smoothed her hands over the tightly bunched muscles in his back, trying to ease the tension that was gripping him.

His arms contracted convulsively. She could hardly breathe. She didn't care.

"I'm going to be a grandfather," he murmured against her temple.

"I know." Val's smile was tender.

"I wanted to be a father again." Longing was woven through his whisper.

"I know." Val closed her eyes against a stinging surge of tears. The moisture clung to the springy hair on his chest. Jonas felt her tears and groaned.

"I love you, Val."

The memory was riding him, terrorizing him; Val could hear it in the tremor in his low voice. "I love you, Jonas." Turning her head, she pressed her parted lips to his moist chest.

"You're a part of me now," he said, responding to her caress with a shiver. "I don't know if I could survive without you. I don't think I'd want to survive." His shiver intensified. "Don't leave me, Val. Don't ever leave me."

"I won't. You know I won't." Val tightened her arms around his waist. "I couldn't."

Jonas was quiet for a moment, his strong arms crushing her softness to him. Val could feel the tension ease out of his taut muscles. A few moments later, she felt a different kind of tension ripple through him. She wasn't at all surprised when he backed her into, then onto, their king-size bed.

This time there was no sense of urgency to Jonas's lovemaking. His kiss was warm, sweet, seductive. Clinging to him, Val returned his kiss fervently. And after three years he knew exactly how to draw passion from her.

His broad hands encased her small, tip-tilted breasts, long fingers stroking the dusky peaks into quivering arousal. The touch of his tongue made her cry out with pleasure and with need. Val arched her back when he drew her into his mouth, and shuddered in response to his hungry suckling.

When Jonas brought his mouth back to hers, Val wrenched a receptive moan and shudder from him by gliding her palms down his torso and encasing him in her hands.

"Oh, Lord, Val, don't stop!" Jonas groaned, as she lightly danced her fingers along his length. His breathing rough, erratic, he endured her ministrations for as long as possible before whispering, "Bring me to you, love."

Once again the tension coiled inside Valerie. And when at last it snapped, she clung to Jonas's solid form to keep from being swept away in the flood of ecstatic release.

Feeling warm and replete, Valerie burrowed close to Jonas as she drifted back to reality. She made a purr-like sound and arched luxuriously in response to the hand that was stroking her from shoulder to hip.

"We're fantastic together," Jonas murmured, gliding his palm to the base of her spine. "Aren't we?"

"Yes." Val smiled in appreciation of the soothing care he never failed to give to her in the afterglow of their lovemaking.

"And you love me?" he asked in a low-pitched voice, continuing his ministrations.

"Yes," Val breathed, again moving luxuriously against him, basking in his attention.

"And you promise never to leave me?" Jonas whispered, trailing his fingers slowly up her body to capture and tease one quivering breast.

"Yes." Val shivered in response to the tormenting stroke of his fingers.

"And you'll forget this nonsense about going to San Francisco without me?" he asked softly.

Floating on the sensuous web Jonas had woven around her, Val was about to murmur one more yes, when his question registered. Another fact registered, as well. Jonas had set out with calculated intent to bemuse and confuse her into capitulating to his wishes!

"No!" Forgetting his warning and her own contrition of a short time ago, Val administered a smart smack to his exposed flank. "Darn you, Jonas!" she exclaimed. Ignoring his grunt of pain, she scrambled away from him. He reached for her, but she avoided his hands by rolling off the side of the bed. "You're trying to manipulate me, and I don't like it."

"Valerie, come back here," Jonas barked, as she stormed toward the bathroom.

Unaware of the alluring picture she made standing framed in the doorway, Val spun around and planted her hands on her hips. "Is that an order, Mr. Thorne, sir?" Arching her raven's-wing eyebrows disdainfully, Val raised her chin and glared at him with outraged defiance.

With the agility of a much younger man, Jonas leaped from the bed and stalked after her. "Damn it, Val, will you wait a minute?" he growled when she turned and dashed into the bathroom.

"For what?" she retorted. "To give you time to think up some other method of persuasive control?" She swung the door closed, but was a heartbeat too slow. The palm of Jonas's hand caught the door a hairbreadth from the frame.

"I'm not trying to control you," he said, forcing her to retreat before the pressure he was applying to the door.

"Ha!" Val exclaimed in ridicule. "In one manner or another, you've exerted control over me from the day we met." She gave a sharp shake of her head, then corrected herself. "No. You were in control long before we actually met."

Jonas sliced one hand through the air with a gesture of dismissal. "I was your employer. The control I had then was minimal."

"Yes, when I first came to work for you, and when I worked in your Paris office," Val conceded. "But you have been in control, in one form or another, ever since you brought me back to the States with you three years ago."

Jonas had the look of a man teetering on the brink of losing his patience. "You needed someone to take control when I brought you back from France," he retorted. "At the time, you were barely able to think straight, let alone make the simplest decision for yourself.''

Stung, because his harsh assertion was true, and she hated being reminded of the state she'd been in back then, Valerie was forced to take several deep, calming breaths to keep from shouting at him.

Her heaving chest drew his narrowed gaze and kindled a flame of renewed arousal in his flinty eyes. ''If I've imposed my will over you or exerted control, it has been for your own welfare.'' A revealing tightness strained his voice.

Valerie was not flattered; she was furious. ''How diligent and thoughtful of you,'' she said with exaggerated sweetness. Quivering in reaction to the anger searing through her, she drew herself up to her full height and glared directly into his eyes. ''Well, Mr. Thorne, sir,'' she continued in a scathing tone, ''your diligence is no longer required. I am now able to think as straight as the next person—man or woman—and I am fully capable of making my own decisions, thank you.''

''Damn it, Val!'' Jonas raked his hand through his hair. ''I never said you weren't capable.''

''I'm delighted to hear it,'' she said grittily. ''Because my decision is made. I am going to San Francisco next month . . . *with* or *without* your approval!''

Jonas stared at her in cold fury, his expression frozen, his mouth tight. Val returned his stare until she thought she'd scream, just to break the tension crackling in the small space that separated them. When at last he broke the silence, his voice was hard, dismissive, hurtful.

"Do what the hell you want." Turning, Jonas stormed from the room, slamming the door behind him with deliberate force.

Val had to bite her lip to stop herself calling out after him. She took a step forward, then stopped. Not this time, she thought, shaking her head sharply. She would not run after Jonas this time. She had been that route before...almost exactly three years before. That time, her impulsive action had cost her the life of her child. This time it might cost her the budding life of her individuality.

But he had looked so alone in his fierceness.

Stop it, Val ordered herself. Just stop it right there. If Jonas now felt alone, it was because he had withdrawn, removed himself from the trials and tribulations of everyday life. If he didn't see the pain and striving of those closest to him, it was because he refused to look, observe, become involved.

It hurt to become involved. Val sighed. She was living proof of how very much it hurt to become involved. She had gone through the process not once, but twice.

Strange how the memory of her first experience with pain had paled into insignificance with the advent of her love for Jonas, Val mused, as she turned on the taps and adjusted the water temperature. Stepping into the stall, she stood directly under the shower spray. The warm water cascaded over her tired body, easing the tension from her mind and muscles.

Her first involvement.

Etienne.

The name whispered through her mind, bringing a bittersweet smile to Val's lips. Absently lathering shampoo into her hair, she slipped into a reverie about the man she had almost married.

Val had loved the gentle, elegant Frenchman, handsome brother of the equally handsome Jean-Paul. And Etienne had died. Val had watched him die. At the time, she had truly believed that all her hopes and dreams for the future had died with him.

Despondent, Val had wallowed in her grief for nearly a year, listless, without interest in the world around her, not caring either for herself or for the effect her carelessness was having on the Paris office of J.T. Electronics.

Then Jonas Thorne himself had flown into Paris, bringing with him Janet Peterson—and the winds of change. When he'd flown out again, back to Philadelphia, Jonas had taken with him a very unwilling Valerie.

And Valerie had felt an immediate and surprising antipathy toward Jonas Thorne.

Val's bittersweet smile curved wryly as she turned off the water and stepped from the shower. How she had resented the man's dynamic personality. His arrogance. His impatience. And his indifference. Even in the numbed state her mind had been in, Val had experienced an unprecedented surge of resentment for her cold-eyed employer.

Now, three years later, Val could smile with amused remembrance of how those feelings had quickly evolved, first into respect, then into admiration for Jonas. It had been because of her growing respect that she had allowed him to talk her into a mutually convenient proposition of marriage.

Smoothing a delicately scented lotion into every inch of skin she could reach, Val winced as she recalled the spineless twit she had been. But then, she mused thoughtfully, even a strong-willed woman wouldn't have stood much of a chance against the determined Jonas. Not three years ago. Not today, either, come to think of it.

Val laughed softly to herself as she recapped the bottle, then wiped the excess lotion from her hands. In her now expert opinion, holding out against Jonas was like trying to halt the incoming tide or attempting to stop a tank with your bare hands.

When Jonas Thorne set his sights on something, be it a business deal or a woman, he played hardball. And when he was in high gear, both the weak and the strong had better head for the hills.

In high gear, Jonas Thorne was a sight to behold. Nobody knew it better than the woman he slept with.

And, having slept with Jonas for over three years, Valerie knew him very well—not completely, not entirely, and definitely not as well as she'd like, but very well indeed.

Val had thought Jonas was operating in high gear when he had unceremoniously whisked her back to the States from France. She had thought the same when he had overridden all her objections and talked her into marrying him. In retrospect, Val realized that in both endeavors Jonas had been merely coasting. Valerie had only seen Jonas shift into high gear the morning after she had slept with him for the first time.

They had been married less than twenty-four hours and were ostensibly on their honeymoon. Jonas had received an early-morning phone call, informing him of an impending business fight. The phone call had catapulted him into high gear and had put an end to their honeymoon.

Val had always believed that if they had had more time alone together, away from the pressures and stress of Jonas's work, they might have avoided the disastrous results of misunderstanding. But they hadn't had that time.

The business battle had raged for over a month, and Jonas had revealed a new facet of his character. When he was mad, really mad, Jonas was a powerhouse of energy, and he swore like a dockworker.

In awe and a little fearful of him, Valerie had kept her suspicions of being pregnant to herself. He had enough to contend with, she'd reasoned, without the added distraction of wondering about a possibility that might prove false with her very next normal cycle.

But then, immediately following his triumph in the business war, Jonas sprang the news on Val that his daughter would be returning home from the school she had been attending in Switzerland . . . on the same day that he was expecting the arrival of a liaison from the offices of a French business associate.

Even now, three years later, Valerie cringed inwardly at the memory of that disastrous day. For when Jonas returned to the house from collecting Mary Beth at the airport, he had with him her mother Lynn, his former wife. And as Val swiftly realized, the still-beautiful Lynn was a certified witch. She was also furious that Jonas had remarried, since she had clearly hoped to remarry him herself.

As if the confusion of meeting both Mary Beth and her acid-tongued mother wasn't enough, the French liaison arrived, and just happened to be Etienne's brother, Jean-Paul.

If they had had time alone together! Val had to laugh at the thought. She had known that Jonas had offered to house the liaison until he could secure a place of his own. But she had been stunned to discover that Lynn would be staying at the house during her visit, as well.

Large though Jonas's home was, Val had suddenly felt that she could hardly move without tripping over somebody. For, besides Jonas, Mary Beth, Lynn, Jean-Paul and Val, there was also Lynn's mother, Marge, who had shared Jonas's home since Mary Beth was an infant.

The mere memory of those tension-filled weeks boggled Val's mind. A chill feathered her naked skin, jolting her out of her introspection.

After slipping a lace and satin nightgown over her head, Val picked up her brush and dryer and turned to face the image reflected in the long mirror above the vanity.

The sodden mass of her black hair was daunting. With a sigh, Val set to work brushing the tangles from the long strands. For years she had worn her naturally curly hair short. But Jonas preferred it long.

The below-shoulder length her hair had attained said reams about how effectively she held out against Jonas, when it came to the crunch.

Not this time, Val vowed to her tight-lipped reflection.

She and Jonas had spent their one-night honeymoon in San Francisco. She had conceived her baby there. Jonas had promised to take her back. He had never mentioned it again.

With a final flip of the brush to her gleaming dry hair, Val set brush and dryer on the vanity. Tilting her chin, she gazed into the mirror and made a promise to herself.

She was going to San Francisco.

Chapter Three

You did what?"

Valerie smiled at the look of astonishment on her companion's face. Janet Peterson had been Val's friend for over ten years, but she had known and worked for Jonas a lot longer. "I said I slapped him," Val repeated.

"Jonas!" Janet exclaimed in a shocked whisper that blended into the muted buzz of the lunchtime conversation from the other patrons, primarily female, in the small suburban Philadelphia restaurant, located within minutes of the home office of J.T. Electronics.

"Twice," Val confessed, omitting to add that the second slap had been to his naked flank.

"Incredible."

"Yes, I know." Val sighed. "I'm still having difficulty believing it myself." Her shoulders moved in a brief, helpless shrug. "I, ah, lost my temper."

"Well, that explains everything." Janet's expression was wry. "You really have changed," she observed, studying Valerie over the rim of the wineglass she'd raised to her lips.

"Have I?" Val frowned.

Janet rolled her eyes. "Are you kidding? Good grief, Val. Two years ago you wouldn't have dreamed of slapping anybody." She gave an abrupt laugh and shook her head. "Now you've slapped Jonas? Yes, I'd say you have changed quite a bit."

Valerie gnawed on her lower lip while contemplating her friend's opinion. She had suffered pangs of remorse and regret for striking Jonas through every one of the four days since that night. She had also suffered stabs from her conscience. Was she becoming too independent and aggressive in her determination to be her own person? More importantly, would she run the risk of losing Jonas if she continued toward the goal of equality that she had set for herself?

On the other hand, Val's emerging assertiveness had countered with the stark declaration that she couldn't revert to the pliable lump of clay she'd been when Jonas had literally taken over her life.

This inner conflict had been Val's primary reason for inviting Janet to lunch. Of all the women Val knew, Janet was the most liberated and sensible. So, if Janet thought she was going too far, Val figured she'd better rethink her game plan.

Of course, Janet hadn't actually said she thought Val was overdoing the feminist bit—only that Val had changed. Deciding to find out how Janet felt, Val went directly to the point.

"In what way have I changed?" she asked. "For the better? Worse? How?"

Janet, being Janet, laughed at Val's blunt demand for answers. "Oh, definitely for the better," she said with conviction. "I'd say you've come pretty much into your own." Her grin was purely feline. "By thinking for yourself, you've not only shaken Jonas up, you've given him something to think about—I mean besides electronics."

Though she felt a measure of relief, Val murmured, "But I shouldn't have hit him."

Janet shrugged. "Probably not...since striking out physically never solves anything." Her expression grew thoughtful. "Did he provoke it?"

"Yes," Val answered without hesitation.

Janet responded with a shrug. "Then don't worry about it. It's not the end of the world, you know."

Val sighed. "But it was rather childish."

"Maybe." Janet eyed her speculatively. "Nevertheless, you have definitely matured."

"I guess everyone needs to grow up sometime, Janet." Val's voice took on a defensive edge. "And, in my case, I'd say it's long overdue. I'm going to be thirty-one years old."

Janet was noticeably unimpressed, but then, it took a great deal to impress Janet. She had often said that her insouciance was a result of Jonas's influence.

"Getting brave in your old age, too, are you?" She arched one eyebrow.

Valerie made a sour face, which was unrelated to the taste of her wine. "No," she admitted.

"Yet you slugged him."

"It was pure reflex." Val set her glass on the table beside her half-eaten salad. "I didn't think... I reacted."

"May one ask what provocation you reacted to?"

A spark of amusement lighted Valerie's eyes. "You mean you can't guess?"

"You told Jonas about your decision to attend that rally or whatever in San Francisco?" Janet asked.

"Yes." Valerie was not about to tell Janet the intimate details, but she felt no compunction at revealing the reason for the argument.

"And might I ask if you're still planning to go?"

"Yes." Val lifted her small chin in defiance.

"Uh-huh." Janet took another sip of her wine, apparently unconcerned. "Then may the bride ask what the chances are of the matron of honor and the best man being on speaking terms on the day of the wedding?" Her smile revealed a tiny crack in her outward composure. "Just curious, you know, since the wedding is only two weeks from tomorrow."

Val's defiance gave way to concern. A tired-sounding sigh whispered through her soft lips. "Oh, Janet, of course we'll be on speaking terms." Val sent up a silent prayer that she could make good on the promise. "You know neither one of us would do anything to ruin your wedding day."

"I sincerely hope not—" Janet's smile was tinged with self-mockery "—considering how long it's taken me to work up the courage to face the altar and the idea of spending each and every one of my remaining days with a man."

"Charlie loves you," Val said with utter conviction.

Janet smiled. "I know. And I love him. But loving each other and living together in holy wedlock are two entirely different concepts."

"Tell me about it," Val rejoined wryly. "But at least you won't need to work through a drastic change of image," she added. "Charlie fell in love with a strong-willed woman. Jonas believed he had married a marshmallow."

"Jonas did marry a marshmallow. Poor Jonas." Janet's grin belied her words.

Valerie made a face. "Poor Jonas my foot. I think poor, arrogant Jonas is long overdue for a mental shaking. I love the man to distraction," she readily admitted. "But I'm tired of playing the boring echo to his voice of authority."

"Love him to distraction?" Janet laughed. "I think you just might *drive* him to distraction."

Val shrugged. "It'll do him good. He's never been there. He might even learn what all the rest of us mortals have to contend with day after day."

"I wouldn't make book on it," Janet drawled, unconsciously echoing one of Jonas's stock expressions. "But meanwhile," she said, glancing at her wristwatch, "I have to get back to the office and contend with the meeting Jonas scheduled for two o'clock this afternoon." She reached for the check, then smiled when Val scooped it from beneath her fingers. "Thanks for lunch," she said as she slid her chair away from the table. "Where are you headed to from here? One of your classes?"

"Nope." Val set her black hair swirling with a brief shake of her head. "I'm armed with plastic and I'm going shopping for some new clothes to take with me to California. I saw a gown in Bloomingdale's that I'm considering for the formal reception that's being held on the last night of the rally. It's a trifle daring." Her smile was sweet. "Jonas will probably blow a fuse when I show it to him."

Janet's ripple of delighted laughter turned heads in the elegant restaurant. "You are living dangerously, aren't you?" she said as they left the establishment.

"It adds spice to life," Val replied. It had certainly spiced up her love life, she thought, recalling Jonas's ardor on the night of their confrontation. To be sure, Jonas hadn't touched her since that night, but . . .

"Will you be at class tonight?" Janet asked, interrupting Val's thoughts.

"Yes, of course."

"Okay, see you then. But right now, I've got to run." With a flashing smile Janet dashed for her car, which she'd parked beside Val's on the restaurant's parking lot.

Despite her protests at the time against his extravagance, Val loved the silver Cadillac Jonas had given her on their first Christmas together. A soft, faintly sad smile curved her mouth as she slid onto the plush leather seat behind the steering wheel.

She had been infinitely more amenable then, Val mused, recalling that holiday morning. Jonas had made hot, sweet love to her that morning, in quite the same way as he had four nights ago, Val remembered with a shiver.

Forgetting where she was for a moment, Val stared through the windshield, reliving the promise of hope she had felt then, two and a half years ago.

Val had been happy then. She and Jonas had weathered the first stormy months of marriage and the loss of their unborn child. Since their marriage had begun as an unromantic business deal, Val had naturally felt uncertainty and doubt about Jonas's feelings for her. With the intention of ending their union, Val had left him a few weeks after suffering her miscarriage.

But she couldn't stay away.

A reminiscent smile shadowed Val's eyes and mouth. Even then, confused and unsure of the feelings, if any, Jonas had for her, Val had loved him to the exclusion of all else, even her own sense of self-protection. Giving in to her own needs, she had returned to Jonas, determined to salvage their marriage if at all possible. Jonas's reaction to her return and her own willingness to make the union work had made the possibilities for their future together seem endless.

Jonas had said he loved her. His declaration was all that Val required . . . at that point in time.

And Val had been happy.

But as the months passed, and she failed to conceive again, Val's happiness began to dissipate, to be replaced by feelings of inadequacy and discontent.

A wealthy man, Jonas showered luxuries on her, beginning with the silver Cadillac and culminating, but certainly not ending, with the house they now occupied. What Jonas didn't understand, couldn't seem to understand, was that although she appreciated and enjoyed every one of his generous gifts, Val didn't need *things*. She needed a sense of purpose, of contribution, of partnership.

Since she had fulfilled the very demanding duties as Jonas's private secretary before their marriage, and was qualified to be the assistant to almost any CEO, Val decided to go back to work. But when she told him about her plans, Jonas swiftly scotched her aspirations.

His objections were valid; Jonas's objections, as well as his objectives, were always valid. He reminded her, unnecessarily, that he himself put in long hours of work each and every day of the week...in addition to quite a few nights. He pointed out to Val that their time together was precious, because it was limited.

Furthermore, although Jonas believed in and supported the principle of equal opportunity for women, and had proved his support by placing several women, Janet included, in executive positions within his company, he stated arrogantly and unconditionally that he wanted his wife in his home. Period. And, as far as Jonas was concerned, the subject was closed.

Acceding to his wishes, Val drifted through life month after endless month, playing the role of housewife and hostess, while plaguing her obstetrician with questions about her seeming inability to conceive a child.

The harried physician ran test after test, all of which proved negative. He then had her doing the morning temperature routine, also to no avail. When he ran out of tests and other ideas, the doctor finally offered the opinion that Val was too tense and too stressed about the whole thing, and advised her to find something to concentrate on other than her inability to become pregnant.

That had been nearly a year ago. Since then, Val had followed the doctor's advice with the fervor born of desperation. It had been a hit-or-miss endeavor. And her first attempt had turned out to be an unmitigated disaster.

Val laughed aloud as she turned the key in the ignition, firing the engine into a well-tuned purr.

She had joined the community garden club, only to learn that she had a thumb as black as her hair, capable of knocking off the heartiest of plants within days of purchase.

Switching on the car radio, Val hummed along with the music as she drove off the parking lot and onto the highway leading to a nearby shopping mall. Along with the soothing melody, memories wafted through her mind as she drove.

Undaunted after the garden club fiasco, Val had enrolled in an eclectic cooking course being offered by a local department store. She was more talented in cooking and, as a result, Jonas suddenly discovered better fare at the dinner table.

He didn't object, Val recalled. On the contrary, Jonas was lavish with his praise. Of course, she mused wryly, preparing excellent meals went hand in glove with housewifery...not to mention with his healthy appetite.

Jonas's objections came later.

Had his initial grumblings of disapproval begun with the course she had taken on emerging female supremacy? Or had they started with the first overnight trip she'd taken away from home as a new member of the local chapter of the Ideas for a Saner World Society?

Val couldn't remember, but she did recall Jonas's opinion of the society in general.

"I think the whole idea is insane," he'd growled. "I'd bet a year of the company's profits that the society was founded by bored women looking for something to do and an excuse to travel while they're doing it."

He was right, of course. Val quickly lost interest in the disorganized organization and the petty squabbling the women indulged in. But while admitting that Jonas was right about the society, Val realized his reasoning on the subject of women was faulty.

In truth, most of the women Valerie had come into contact with in the course of her varied pursuits *were* bored. But, she reflected, had anyone ever bothered to delve into the reason why they were bored? As far as Val could ascertain, no one had...most especially not the women's own husbands.

Although Val had met women who were plainly just malcontents, the majority was happily married to men with high incomes, men who took pride in their ability to support and maintain their families, men who preferred their wives not to have careers. In other words, Valerie met housewives who needed something more, women exactly like herself.

A blast of rock and roll from the radio jolted Val out of her reverie just as she was about to drive by the last entrance lane into the mall.

Cursing under her breath at her inattention, Val made the turn in the nick of time, telling herself to get her head together and keep it that way.

At midafternoon on a Friday, the mall was full, mainly of women with small children. Dodging the baby strollers, Val concentrated on her business. The reason she had given Janet for her expedition was true... up to a point. Val did intend to shop for a few things to take to California. But her main objective was to pick up the engraved sterling silver service she had ordered as a wedding gift for Janet and Charlie.

Leaving the gift for last, Val browsed through several of the stores, vacillating in her mind over the gown she had mentioned to Janet. After forty-odd minutes of indecision, and telling herself Jonas really would explode if she came home with the dress, Val straightened her shoulders and marched into the large department store. Some thirty or so minutes later she left the mall, the silver, several accessory items and the gown in hand.

The phone was ringing when Val let herself into the house through the garage entrance. Dumping her handbag, car keys and packages onto the table, she dashed across the room and grabbed the kitchen extension.

"Hello," she panted in a breathless voice.

"Where did I chase you from?" Marge, Jonas's former mother-in-law, asked in her usual down-to-earth manner.

"Oh, hi, Marge," Val said, in between taking deep breaths. "I just came in from shopping."

"Did you buy yourself some goodies?" the older woman asked, bringing a smile to Val's mouth. Marge, as Val well knew, was a dedicated window shopper.

"A gown to die for," Val answered, her smile growing into an impish grin. "Jonas will likely need to hire a roofer after he gets a look at it."

"Go through the ceiling, will he?" Marge said with a laugh.

"I'm afraid so," Val replied in a dry tone.

"Good," Marge snorted. "The cracker needs to be jostled out of his rut every now and again."

Val chuckled at the older woman's use of the nickname the people closest to Jonas used to describe him. Having originally come from Tamaqua in the Pennsylvania coal region, Jonas had acquired the appellation of "coal cracker" somewhere along the way from bastard orphan to business titan.

Reminded of him, Val slanted a glance at the clock. "And, speaking of the cracker," she drawled. "I'd better get cracking with dinner."

"And speaking of dinner," Marge echoed. "That's the reason I called. Tomorrow night. Seven-thirty."

"I hadn't forgotten, Marge." Val groaned silently. Excited about becoming a great-grandmother in the near future, Marge had insisted on preparing a family celebration dinner, which by itself didn't bother Val.

The hitch was that Marge had also insisted on including Lynn in the party. "Is there something I can do to help?" she asked, resigned to the ordeal.

"No, thank you. I have everything under control."

Val had to laugh. "You always do. But if you find you need some help, give me a call."

"Under the circumstances, that's very generous of you." The older woman's voice was thick with emotion. "You're a real lady, Valerie."

"Thank you," Val said, then blurted out without thinking, "That's nice, but can you tell me why it seems that the real ladies of this world have to fight for everything twice as hard as the real bitches?"

"No, I can't," Marge replied. "But remember, you have Jonas, Val."

And Lynn doesn't. The unspoken rider hummed along the line connecting the two phones.

"Yes, I have Jonas," Val said. *The problem is to hold the marriage together without surrendering unconditionally,* she reflected with wry humor. Keeping her thoughts to herself, she continued smoothly, "And Jonas and I will be there tomorrow evening."

"I do understand how difficult this will be for you, Val," Marge said, making it clear that she saw through Val's smooth tone. "And I want you to know how much I appreciate it. Some women...a lot of women...would have raised a fuss, if not flat out refused to show up."

"Well," Val said, "I won't promise that I'll be there with bells on, but I will be there."

"Because you're nice," Marge said.

Or stupid, Val thought. Or a coward. Or both. Aloud she merely said, "It's nice to know you think I'm nice, but right now, I have to get a move on. See you tomorrow, Marge."

Val shot another glance at the clock as she hung up. Time was gaining on her, and she had a lot to do before leaving for the exercise class she attended twice a week with Janet. As it was, she probably wouldn't have time to eat dinner, especially if Jonas was late getting home, which he was more often than not.

Being careful of the large white bow on the elaborately wrapped gift, Val collected her packages, carried them to the bedroom and deposited them on the bed. After changing into lightweight slacks and a tailored shirt, she returned to the kitchen to prepare dinner.

Jonas was late. He was tired. He was in a conciliatory mood. But, as luck would have it, he had, as usual, forgotten that it was Val's night for exercise class.

"What's the rush?" he asked idly, observing her hurried activity from the doorway.

Val continued to stir the cheese sauce for the vegetables as she cast a look at him. "I hope you don't mind sitting at the breakfast counter to eat," she said, avoiding his eyes and his question.

"I don't." Jonas strolled to the stove. Looming over her, he sniffed appreciatively. "Smells good." Dipping his head, he nuzzled the curve of her shoulder. "So do you."

While Val's senses soared, her spirits plummeted. Why now? she groaned inwardly. During the past four days she had been waiting and hoping for his mood to improve. By why did it have to be now? She trembled visibly when his teeth gently raked her soft skin. Feeling her tremor, he murmured her name and slid his arms around her waist.

"Jonas." Forgetting the sauce, Val turned into his arms and raised her mouth for his kiss.

His mouth was hotter than the burners on the stove. His kiss gave silent testimony to the hunger raging inside his body. "I need you, Val," he groaned against her mouth. "It's been four days, and that's three and a half too many. Let's postpone dinner for an hour or so."

"Oh, Jonas, I can't," Val cried, pulling away from him.

"Why not?" Jonas inquired with a frown.

"I have to leave in a few minutes to meet Janet," Val replied.

"For what?" he demanded.

Anger born of impatience sharpened Val's voice. "It's Friday, Jonas. My exercise class... Remember?"

"Oh, hell," he muttered. Frustration scored his strong features. "I was looking forward to a quiet evening alone with you."

Weakening, Val glanced at the clock. If she could catch Janet at home, Val was positive she wouldn't mind if—

"Why don't you give the class a skip?" Jonas muttered, interrupting her thoughts. "You don't need the damned exercise, anyway. You're thin as a rail now."

Thin as a rail! That did it, Val thought, moving away from the stove. "No, Jonas, I can't give it a skip. I told Janet I'd be there." Stiff with anger, Val walked to the closet to get her purse and gym bag.

"Hey!" Jonas exclaimed. "What about dinner?"

Val paused at the door to level a cool look at him. She was tempted to tell him precisely what he could do with the meal. Instead she said, "Since you're going to eat it, you can damn well finish cooking it yourself."

As a rule, Val enjoyed the exercise class. Tonight was the exception. Seething with anger and resentment at Jonas's lack of interest for practically everything unconnected to electronics, she performed the routines automatically, stretching and flexing her mind more than her body as she inwardly raged against his attitude. By the time the class was over, Val was physically exhausted and mentally depleted.

"God, I hate this class," Janet grumbled as they changed from their leotards into street clothes. "I keep wondering why I do this to myself two nights a week."

"To stay trim, supple and young looking," Val replied in a tired mutter.

"Right." Janet grimaced. "You know, Val, there are days, many in number, when I feel like saying to hell with all this silliness." She raked a brush through the hair she had allowed to grow to shoulder length because Charlie liked long hair on a woman. "I mean," she added, tossing the brush into her nylon carryall, "do you ever get the feeling that what you have to go through to stay trim, supple and young

looking is rather ridiculous . . . considering that in the
end you lose the battle to old age, anyway?''

Some of Val's resentment seeped through her guard.
"Why, Janet Peterson, surely you're not suggesting we
let ourselves go to pot and simply enjoy life?''

Janet eyed her shrewdly as they left the building and
headed for the parking lot. "You're tired of it, too,
huh?''

Val sighed. "Not the exercises. I usually enjoy the
workout. I suppose I'm just in a bad mood tonight.''

Janet stopped beside Val's car. "And I suppose I'm
just having pre-wedding jitters." Her grin was unrepentant. "But I still hate the exercises." She started to
move toward her own car, then paused to ask, "By the
way, did you buy that gown you were telling me
about?''

"Yes.''

"What did Jonas say?''

"Nothing.''

"Really!" Janet exclaimed. "Incredible.''

"He hasn't seen it yet," Val admitted.

"Well, good luck, with Jonas and with Lynn tomorrow night." With a grin and a wave, Janet turned
away. "If the witch gives you a hard time, haul off and
belt her. No one deserves it more." Her laughter
wafted back to Val on the warm spring air.

Valerie mulled over Janet's parting sally all the way
home. And the more she mulled it over, the madder
she got.

Without a shadow of a doubt, Val knew that Jonas
would have a fit when she showed him the dress. The
realization rankled.

Why shouldn't she buy any damn dress she wanted? she asked herself irritably. Why shouldn't any woman, come to that? Men bought and wore whatever they chose, didn't they?

So the dress was a little daring, she railed. So what. It certainly didn't overstep the bounds of decency, and she looked pretty terrific in it, if she did say so herself.

Oh, but she knew, knew too well what Jonas would say, Val thought, kicking her anger into high gear. He'd very likely give her that cold, arrogant look of his and ask her what kind of game she was planning to stalk.

What was it with the male of the species, anyway? Val fumed. What was it in their thinking process that prevented them from affording the female the same rights as they demanded for themselves?

And why, when he devoted the majority of his energy and time to his professional pursuits, did Jonas object so strenuously to his wife wanting to plumb the depths of her own capabilities? Now Val carried her furious stream of consciousness to the personal level. Why couldn't he see or understand her need to feel his equal in situations and circumstances other than those requiring a prone position in a bed?

And why should she be expected to endure his former wife's waspish remarks? Val asked herself in outrage. Everyone, from Janet and the rest of Jonas's employees to Jonas himself, knew that Lynn derived pleasure from baiting Val. And, though Jonas generally ignored Lynn and had advised Val to do likewise, she was thoroughly fed up with the tiresome woman.

By the time she made a sharp turn into the driveway, Val had whipped herself into a righteous fury and was spoiling for a fight.

One was waiting for her.

Standing at the bedroom window, Jonas narrowed his eyes as he watched the car's headlights precede the silver Cadillac into the driveway. Behind him, Val's new gown lay in a crumpled heap on the bed, where he had flung it in unbridled anger.

Val had been gone less than three hours, but that was enough time for Jonas to work himself into a jealous rage.

And all because of an innocent, if marginally daring, chiffon confection in the exact same shade of violet as his wife's hauntingly beautiful eyes.

He had discovered the dress while seeking to relieve his boredom. Not that it had been hidden away; it hadn't been. It had been on the bed, still in the distinctive department store box, where Val had obviously placed it on her return from shopping.

Restless after finishing the delicious meal Val had prepared for him, which he had no more than picked at, Jonas had wandered upstairs. His intention had been to work until Val came home, but he never made it into the office. On entering the bedroom, Jonas couldn't help but notice the packages strewed across the bed.

Wryly wishing that he and Val were cluttering the spread instead of the parcels, he idly crossed to the bed and curiously began examining the contents of the assortment of bags and boxes. The wrapped wedding gift brought a grunt of satisfaction from his throat. The skimpy pieces of satin and lace he uncovered in another package brought a smile to his lips and an ache to his loins. The low-cut bodice on the shimmering gown, on the other hand, sent a quiver of uncertainty shafting through him.

The gown was beautiful, and would look even more so draped on Val's sylphlike body. A frown drew Jonas's brows together. Val had never before bought or worn anything quite so suggestive, at least not to his knowledge, and not for him. Why had she purchased this particular gown now? Had she bought it to take with her to San Francisco? Jonas felt positive that she had. The gown was obviously expensive. The price didn't upset Jonas, but Val's reason for buying it did bother him.

With little effort, Jonas could imagine how Val would look with the shimmering dress floating around her ankles and her gorgeous hair swirling around her bared shoulders. The image was so sharp, so appealing that he caught his breath.

But why had she bought the gown to wear when he wouldn't be with her? Jonas asked himself, feeling anger stir. The question repeated itself throughout the hours Val was away.

Intellectually, Jonas knew his anger was unwarranted. But his emotions were running close to the surface. Jonas wasn't feeling intellectual or even logical. He was feeling the sharp claws of jealousy.

Was Val tired of competing with his obsession for his work? Tired enough to seek solace in the attentions of another man? Jonas didn't want to believe that Val would deceive him. But jealousy clouded his thinking and ignited his temper.

All because he had opened a box and found a gown seemingly made for seduction.

Responding to his own unsettling thoughts, Jonas crushed the filmy material in his clenched fists, then flung it away from him.

Jonas was still standing at the window, his expression frozen, when Val entered the bedroom. He didn't turn around until he heard her startled gasp.

"Jonas, what . . . ?" Val's voice trailed away as she ran to the bed.

"What did you buy it for?" he asked, turning to watch her carefully lift the gown from the bed.

The look she sent him held dawning comprehension. Without having to hear him admit to the act, she knew he had deliberately tossed the gown into a heap. "I bought it to wear to the dinner and reception being held the last night of the rally," she replied angrily, examining the dress for possible damage.

"If it's still in one piece," he said, as she held the garment aloft and gently shook it, "take it back."

Val raised her chin in a familiar gesture of defiance. "I most certainly will not take it back. I am taking it to California." Her tone was tight with determination. Crossing to the walk-in closet, she disappeared inside. When she emerged, her hands were empty, and planted on her narrow hips. "And I am going to wear it to the reception." The glitter in her eyes defied him to forbid her to do either.

"Are you planning to come back from California?" Jonas asked, not even certain he wanted to hear her answer to the question that had just occurred to him.

Val's expression went blank an instant, then her eyes flew wide with surprise. "Yes, of course I'm coming back!" she exclaimed. "Why would you even dream that I wouldn't?"

The breath Jonas hadn't realized he was holding eased from his constricted chest. "That dress." He flicked his hand at the closet. "It's the kind of thing a woman wears when she's trying to attract male attention."

Val looked astonished. The next moment, her eyes flashed with anger. Then she exploded. "Jonas Thorne, that is the most ridiculous statement you've ever made! It ranks right up there with the blanket condemnations made by the idiots who maintain that a woman is inviting physical attack by the way she dresses." Moving slowly, she walked to within inches of him. Her voice was soft, but held a steel thread of warning. "Watch yourself, mister. You're getting fast and loose with your accusations...and I'm getting pretty damn tired of hearing them."

She was right. Jonas knew she was right. His remark wasn't merely ridiculous, it was stupid. Jonas didn't like feeling ridiculous and stupid. He didn't like feeling jealous, either. But, since he'd never experienced any of these feelings before falling in love with

Val, Jonas didn't know quite how to back out of the corner he'd talked himself into.

Besides, there was his pride to contend with.

"I haven't accused you of anything," he finally replied. "But you can't blame a man for objecting to his wife parading around half-naked in front of other men when he's not with her." The instant the words were out of his mouth, Jonas knew he was in even deeper trouble.

"Half-naked!" Val erupted like a volcano. "Parade! How dare you! I never parade around in front of men... naked or otherwise." She raised her hand, and Jonas's eyes narrowed in warning. But all she did was tap him on the chest, hard, with her small index finger. "And, for your information, Mr. Thorne, the only reason my husband won't be around is simply because he refuses to accompany his wife."

She scored a bull's-eye. Jonas felt it, but wasn't about to concede the bout. "You never said a word about the damned rally until you called to inform me that you were going to San Francisco. I didn't refuse to accompany you," he shot back. "I wasn't invited along." But Jonas had to admit to himself that had she asked him to go with her, he would have refused, all the while assuming that with his refusal, Val would not go by herself. All the same, when it came to confessing to Val what he admitted to himself, pride got in the way.

"Because I knew you wouldn't go," Val countered.

"Someone has to work to pay for things like cars and jewelry and expensive gowns that are only half there," he retaliated without thinking.

Val literally bristled. "Some*one* wouldn't have to, if he weren't so dead set against his wife working!"

"Don't start that again," Jonas growled, his anger renewed by that old bone of contention. "Why can't you be content just being my wife?"

"Would you be?" Val demanded.

"What?"

"Reverse our positions, Jonas," she said patiently. "Then ask yourself if you'd be content to stay home, twiddling your thumbs and vegetating."

Jonas was outflanked and knew it. He was a fair man and had never treated any woman with less than equality. But he had a blind spot about Val. It had been that way from the beginning. She was exclusively his. He wanted to maintain the status quo.

So, even though he knew intellectually that he was being unfair, Jonas was caught in an emotional web that had been reinforced by ego and pride. By rights, he knew he should back down. Hell, by rights he knew he owed Val an apology. But pride, ego and emotional entanglement dominated. Instead of backing down, Jonas attacked.

"But our positions aren't reversed. I'm not a woman. You are." Lifting his hand, Jonas caught her delicate chin with hard fingers. His voice was harsh with warning. "You are *my* woman. And don't you ever forget it."

Chapter Four

Valerie lay beside Jonas in the big bed, separated from him physically by mere inches, but emotionally by miles. Her body was taut, quivering in reaction to the anger simmering inside her tired mind.

His woman.

The taunt sprang into her mind every time she began to relax, releasing a fresh onslaught of anger. Half an hour had passed since Jonas had coldly informed Val that she belonged to him. The scene following his pronouncement had been replayed inside her head repeatedly during that tense span of time.

"I'm not a thing, Jonas!" Val had cried.

"I didn't say you were. I said you were a woman."

"You said I was *your* woman."

"Well, aren't you?"

"Yes, but . . ."

Jonas's smile was maddeningly triumphant. "End of argument. I'm tired and I'm going to bed."

The memory of the frustration she had experienced, was still experiencing, had Val grinding her teeth. Turning away from her without another word, Jonas had proceeded to undress. Then, sweeping the packages off the bed and dropping them into one of the easy chairs by the window, he crawled between the sheets, leaving her fuming. She had no option but to follow suit.

Val had considered sleeping in the guest room, but rejected the notion out of pure stubbornness. Jonas had had his way once too often, she'd decided, beginning with his insistence that they marry, and ending with his insistence that she remain at home, playing the role of dutiful wife. She had retreated before his commanding personality for the last time. She would not retreat again.

Tossing off her clothes, Val had climbed onto the very edge of the king-size mattress. She had literally clung there, seething, ever since.

"Val?"

His soft voice alerted her an instant before his arm curled around her waist to haul her against his naked body. His *aroused* naked body. Val went stiff with outrage and disbelief. Surely he didn't think she'd . . . ? But of course he did, she thought, incensed. She was *his* woman, wasn't she?

"I love you, Val." Looming over her, Jonas lowered his head to hers.

Val pulled her head away as his mouth brushed hers. "Let me go, Jonas," she ordered through gritted teeth.

Ignoring her command, Jonas slowly glided his palm from her waist to her hip and over her flat belly, taking possession of the soft mound below as he planned to take possession of her whole body... as if by right of ownership.

Passion unfurled deep inside Val, strong and urgent. Fighting her response to his nearness, his touch, she clenched her teeth. She couldn't allow him to do this again, she told herself. She would not! Stiff muscles beginning to grow warm and pliant, she strained against his hold.

Jonas tested her resistance by caressing the corner of her mouth with his parted lips. "The argument's over, ended." A smile hovered on his lips. "Come, love, kiss me, make love with me, it's not like you to sulk," he murmured, inadvertently freeing her from the sensuous spell he alone could induce.

"I'm not sulking." Val's voice was soft, raspy from her effort to control the urge to shout at him.

Mistaking the husky sound for passion, Jonas worked his long fingers between her tightly closed thighs. "Then why don't you relax? Why won't you kiss me?"

"Because I'm mad, Jonas," Val said angrily. "And when I'm mad, I'm mad all over." Clasping his wrist, she pushed his hand away. "Now get your hands off me."

His surprise and shock apparent, Jonas grew absolutely still. Val saw the color seep from his face, then rush back, flaring darkly under the taut skin over his jutting cheekbones.

Staring at him, Val lay rigid and shivering, waiting for his reaction. When it came, it was abrupt and violent. Muttering a string of curses that singed her ears, Jonas threw back the covers and leaped from the bed. Every muscle in his trim, magnificent body taut with tension, he stared down at her from narrowed eyes.

"I'm sorry if my touch is repulsive to you," he said with unrelenting harshness.

Although his set features were devoid of expression, Val could sense the pain of rejection and humiliation he was suffering. Jolting upright, she reached out to him. "Jonas, I didn't say or mean that I find your touch repulsive. I don't. You know I don't. But I can't go on—"

"Spare me the excuses," Jonas interrupted her in a hard tone. "I don't need them." Spinning on his heel, he strode from the room, slamming the door after him.

Val's extended arm fell limply to her thigh and she stared at the door until the tears filling her eyes blurred her vision. She had started to say that she couldn't go on acting as if nothing had happened, while the dissension between them remained unresolved. Why hadn't Jonas listened? More importantly, why didn't he ever *hear* her, even when he did listen?

Chilled on the inside and outside, Val lay down again, this time on Jonas's side of the bed. Suddenly it seemed enormous. Feeling the warmth left from his body, inhaling the masculine scent of him, she curled into a ball of misery beneath the covers. Val rarely gave way to tears. But now she was alone, with no one to see her submit to despair. Burying her face in the indentation made by his head, Val sobbed into Jonas's pillow.

His muscles locked with tension, Jonas lay in the unfamiliar bed, alternately cursing and berating himself for his uncivilized behavior. But though he was disgusted, he was not surprised. He always wound up losing his temper when he and Val argued. Jonas even knew why he always lost his temper with her; the possibility of losing her scared him stupid.

She had rejected him, and that had both scared and hurt Jonas. So he'd reacted true to form by lashing out at her. Then when she had tried to explain her feelings she had scared him even more, because he'd been afraid she was going to say she couldn't go on with him any longer. So he'd cut her off.

He had been hurt, and he'd wanted to hurt her back. Yet now, alone in a strange bed, aching for her in every cell of his body, Jonas was hurting as much for Val as for himself.

Val had ordered him to take his hands off her.

That had been his problem from the first time he saw her. Jonas groaned. He just couldn't keep his hands off her.

Rolling onto his side, Jonas curled into a ball and punched the pillow.

Damn it! Why did being in love have to hurt so much?

The question kept Jonas awake most of the night.

*   *   *

Val awoke early Saturday morning with a hangover from the crying jag in the form of a blasting headache. Feeling as though she'd been on a three-day binge, she dragged her tired body from the bed. She had slept a total of three hours. Her eyes were redrimmed, her mind was dull and her spirits were not merely low but down for the count.

Other than leave her body clean and wet, a stinging shower had little effect upon her condition. After pulling on her regular Saturday attire of jeans, a T-shirt and flat shoes, Val took a few listless swipes at her disheveled hair with a brush before heading downstairs.

The house was quiet. Valerie had become accustomed to the silence. The house was always quiet. Jonas seldom stayed home from the office on Saturday. As a rule, Val woke when he left the bed, then got up to make him breakfast. This morning, she hadn't even heard him moving around.

Val sniffed as she made her way to the kitchen. The aroma was tantalizing. Obviously Jonas had made breakfast for himself before leaving for the office. The scent of coffee drew her like a magnet. Val took a step into the room and came to an abrupt halt, a startled "Oh!" bursting from her parched throat.

Jonas was seated at the breakfast counter, a steaming cup of coffee cradled in his hands. He glanced around at her as she began to move again.

"There's coffee," he said brusquely, jerking his head to indicate the nearly full pot.

"Yes, I see." Val's voice was strained. She wet her dry lips. "Thank you."

"You're welcome," her husband replied.

Like strangers, Val thought, grasping the handle of the coffeepot with trembling fingers. They were acting like strangers, making polite, stilted conversation.

"What would you like for breakfast?" Val tried to infuse some warmth into her voice, and winced when the sound came out flat and dull.

"It doesn't matter." Jonas's tone betrayed a lack of interest.

"I don't know how to cook that." She winced again; her attempt at wry humor was falling as flat as she felt.

"I think you use a frying pan." Instead of teasing, Jonas's voice sounded chiding.

"Right." Val sighed. She was tired, and it was going to be a very long day.

In silence she cooked him scrambled eggs. Jonas ate them in silence. He read the morning paper. She listened to the kitchen clock tick. When he finally spoke, she started.

"I've ordered a half dozen bottles of champagne to be delivered to Marge for tonight."

"That was thoughtful of you."

More silence. Heavy. Oppressive. When Val couldn't stand it another moment, she spoke again. "I picked up the gift for Janet and Charlie yesterday."

"I saw it."

Silence.

When Val had had enough, she decided to fill the quiet with some productive noise. Pushing back her chair, she got up and carried her cup to the sink.

"Where are you going?"

Val's head whipped around at the sharp note in Jonas's voice. "To collect the laundry." She frowned. "Why?"

His shrug looked more stiff than casual. "Would you mind refilling my cup?" As if in afterthought, he picked up the cup and held it out to her. She filled the cup for him, then left the room.

It was a very long day, peppered by awkward attempts at innocuous conversation and obvious avoidance of meaningful discussion.

It was a trying day, at least for Val. Every time she turned around, she nearly ran smack into Jonas, who seemed to be trailing her from room to room as she went about her normal Saturday routine of straightening the house, while the laundry went through the wash and dry cycles.

Lunch proved to be a reenactment of breakfast—silence, intermittently broken by stilted remarks. Val had never faced the cleaning up with such relief.

Late in the afternoon, Jonas suggested a nap. Val told him to go right ahead. After staring at her for tautly strung seconds, Jonas turned away from her.

Watching him with pain-filled eyes, Val fought against the clamoring desire to run after him, burrow into the secure haven of his strong arms and agree to any demands he might make of her, be they for then or the future.

Her eyes closed in time with the bedroom door. She had won the inner battle. But had she lost the marriage war?

Val felt beat. Three hours of sleep followed by ten hours of busywork, tension and dodging the issues were not conducive to a party mood. The last thing she felt like doing was getting ready to go out. Nevertheless, get ready she did, and with attention to detail, at that.

Faced with the unavoidable necessity of socializing with the acid-tongued Lynn, Val donned full battle array. Her tiny-flower-strewed, crinkle silk dress enhanced the color of her eyes, displayed her slender figure to best advantage, and was in perfect taste for the occasion. Her narrow, three-inch heels increased her height, added length to her slim legs and drew the eye to her delicate ankles. Employing the expertise she had acquired in Paris, Val deftly highlighted her eyes, cheekbones and mouth. Her gold filigree necklace and earrings had been custom made to Jonas's design. The elusive scent surrounding her sold for over two hundred dollars an ounce.

When she had finished, Jonas's expression alone was worth every minute of the time she'd invested. By the same token, Val felt certain her own expression of admiration mirrored his. Attired in a business suit, Jonas didn't merely look terrific. In semiformal midnight blue against a stark white knife-pleated shirt, he was nothing short of devastating.

"New dress?" Jonas asked, in what sounded like a croak.

"Yes." Val raised her arms to swirl the matching stole around her shoulders; his narrowed gaze followed the gentle lift and sway of her silk-draped breasts.

"I like it." His voice grew low. "It looks beautiful...on you."

Val told herself that she couldn't care less whether he approved of her choice or not, but knew she was lying. She told herself she didn't care if he thought she looked beautiful, but knew she did. The proof was in the sudden lack of strength in her entire body.

Silence filled the car throughout the five-mile drive to the house Valerie had entered as a bride, which Jonas had signed over to Mary Beth and Jean-Paul when their residence he had had built for Val and himself was completed.

Tension crackled in the air between them. Val's mind wandered into deep, dark waters.

He looked good. She looked good. They were good together in a social situation. They were even better together in bed. So what were they doing driving in emotion-fraught silence to a dinner that obviously neither of them wanted to eat? Why weren't they at home, in bed, feasting on each other?

"Hungry?"

Val started. Warmth suffused her cheeks. Had she spoken her longing? Jonas's voice had been too soft for her to detect any inflection...or insinuation. She would have to look at him to know. Slowly Val turned to gaze at his profile. A sigh of relief whispered through her lips; the stern expression he had worn all day was still in place. Jonas was once more making polite conversation.

"Ah...a little." Val's voice was barely there. "You?"

Jonas was at least honest. "Not particularly."

Silence. Again. And for what seemed like forever....

Jonas shattered the quiet as he brought the car to a stop in the driveway of their destination. "Marge did tell you that Lynn would be here this evening?" he asked, rather belatedly, Val thought.

"Yes, she told me."

He killed the engine and turned to look at her. "I'd appreciate it if you'd try to ignore Lynn if she runs to type with her sugar-coated barbs," he said, in a way that had the overtones of an order. Bristling, Val was on the verge of telling him what he could do with his appreciation, when he saved himself by adding, "I don't want Mary Beth upset at this stage of her pregnancy." The dark specter of memory shaded his tone. "Do you?"

Val felt a stab of pain deep in her womb. "No," she answered in a tight murmur.

"Good." Jonas pulled at the car door handle, then paused to shoot a hard look at her. "Do you think you could manage a smile and pretend that you're happy being married to me?" A cynical smile tugged at one corner of his mouth. "I'd hate it like hell if Lynn suspected we were anything but deliriously happy." The smile struggled across his mouth. "She'd laugh her brainless head off." Without waiting for her to respond, Jonas shoved the door open and stepped out of the car.

By the time Jonas circled the car, Val had opened her own door and was about to get out. Accepting the hand he extended to help her, she stepped out and spoke out at the same time. "Are you planning on joining in on this pretense?"

Careful of her dress, Jonas shut the door before answering. "Of course."

"Very well." Slipping her arm through his, Val moved with him to the house. An instant before the front door was swung open for them, she glanced up to give him a brilliant smile. "Let's go bamboozle Lynn."

As he entered the house Jonas was laughing, the rich, warm laughter that never failed to dissolve Val's bones. She clung to his arm in reaction to the melting sensation.

"Hi, Dad," Mary Beth called as they strolled into the spacious living room. "What's the joke?"

The look Jonas gave Val could have sizzled bacon. "It's a private...personal joke, honey," he replied to his daughter, while gazing at his wife.

"Jonas," Val murmured, following his lead.

"Hmm?" Jonas murmured.

"We're not alone." Val had difficulty in keeping her voice husky and her laughter contained. To her amazement, she was enjoying their charade.

"Ain't it a bitch?"

"He always did swear like a seasoned marine," Lynn said in a scathing tone.

Thinking the words applied better to Lynn, Val turned her head to offer the still-beautiful, voluptuous woman a sweet smile. "At times," she said, her lashes sweeping down as she cast a sideways glance at Jonas, "he even makes love like a seasoned marine."

Jonas's burst of laughter was echoed by everyone in the room except Lynn. She narrowed her eyes.

"Perhaps you should get a scrap of paper and take notes, my pet," Jean-Paul advised Mary Beth. "It would appear that Valerie could give lessons on the exquisite art of stroking a husband's fragile ego."

Mary Beth looked at her husband, at Val, then she frowned. "Why is it," she mused aloud, "that everything a Frenchman says sounds so much sexier than even the most seductive whispers of other men?"

Pretending to consider the question, Val moved to sit in the corner of the long sofa. "I don't know," she said, primly folding her hands in her lap.

Jean-Paul was chuckling as only a Frenchman can.

Lynn was scowling.

Marge was grinning.

Sauntering to the sofa, Jonas sat down next to Val and cocked a brow at his daughter. "Forget the scrap of paper, kid," he drawled. "You require no lessons on the art of stroking your husband's ego."

"Or anything else, come to think of it," Jean-Paul said, sharing a secret smile with his wife.

"Disgusting!" Lynn said, grimacing.

"Disgusting, *madame*?" Jean-Paul raised his eyebrows, his expression betraying the disdain he normally kept scrupulously concealed.

"Mother, really." Mary Beth sighed.

"They're only teasing, Lynn," Marge chided.

Biting back a retort, Val remained silent.

His expression cool, Jonas turned his head to look at his former wife. "There is never anything disgusting about love, or the expression of it," he rebuked her in a voice threaded with steel.

There was a moment of tension while Lynn tried to outstare Jonas. The moment ended when she glanced away. In an odd way, Val sympathized with the other woman. Val had experienced the freezing effect of a quelling stare from Jonas's icy eyes.

"May I offer you a drink, Valerie, Jonas?" Jean-Paul's smoothly inserted question banished the chill. "A glass of your generous gift, perhaps?"

Jonas shifted to glance at Marge. "When were you planning to serve dinner?"

Marge smiled, revealing the affection and respect she held for him. "Ten minutes after you arrived," she replied.

Jonas grinned, and turned his attention back to his son-in-law. "Since dinner is about to be announced, I'll wait." He raised a brow at Val. "Darling?"

Jonas had called her darling many times over the previous three years, but the sound of the endearment still had the power to interfere with her normal heartbeat. "No, thank you." She smiled at Jean-Paul as she stood up. "I'm going to help Marge serve dinner."

"How sweet." Lynn's sour expression betrayed her feelings only too well. "You play your role very well, don't you, dear?"

Valerie froze, and checked an urge to look at Jonas. Had Lynn somehow seen through their pretense? Holding on to her outward composure, Val met the other woman's envy-ridden eyes. "I beg your pardon?"

"Your role of devoted housewife," Lynn said disparagingly. "The little woman who keeps her husband's house, and cooks his meals, and washes his dirty laundry."

Relief shivered through Val. "I'm not playing a role, Lynn, I'm living a life," she said with pride. "And I consider being Jonas's wife a lifetime commitment." Val refrained from adding that it was too bad that Lynn hadn't felt the same while she was married to Jonas.

Minutes later, while she was carrying the meat platter to the table, Val caught Jonas staring at her with eyes that revealed both longing and reproach. Her boast to Lynn resounded in her mind, and her feelings of relief and pride changed to remorse and shame. Averting her eyes, she placed the platter on the table and returned to the kitchen.

While chatting with Marge and generally making herself useful, Val suffered the relentless stabs of her conscience. She had spent months pursuing self-understanding and rebelling against being considered nothing more than a wife and homemaker. Yet she had defended that very position to Lynn only moments ago.

Telling herself that she was only keeping her promise to Jonas didn't ease her sense of guilt. Val knew that the sincerity in her tone when she'd made the statement was genuine; she had believed every word she'd uttered.

For most of the meal Val was distracted. Although she heard every word spoken around the table, and responded when someone spoke directly to her, inside her head Val was struggling with her thoughts.

Was it possible to believe that accepting the position of wife and making that lifetime commitment could coexist with a woman's right to grow and expand to her full potential? Didn't the latter cancel out the former, or vice versa?

But she wanted it both ways! The realization jolted through Val, shedding light on her confusion. Raising her flute, she sipped her champagne and slanted a surreptitious glance at her husband's face. As always, merely looking at his rugged, harshly chiseled face caused a flutter of excitement in her midsection.

Jonas Thorne was one exciting man, Val mused. He was formidable but exciting. And she loved him so much that it scared her at times. But it wasn't only a matter of loving Jonas, she concluded. She loved being his wife, with all the responsibilities that entailed.

Val dredged up the memory of Lynn's cynical taunt for a closer examination.

Devoted housewife. The little woman who keeps her husband's house, and cooks his meals, and washes his dirty laundry.

Yes, Val acknowledged, the description fitted her to a capital *T* and in truth, she enjoyed keeping his house, cooking his meals, and even washing his dirty laundry. Val knew that while she told herself she didn't want a housekeeper because she needed to feel that she was contributing something to the marriage, she was deluding herself. She kept house simply because she enjoyed keeping house for Jonas.

On the other hand, Val admitted to herself that she also enjoyed the outside activities she'd become involved with in her determination to discover the limits of her own capabilities as a mature individual.

So she wanted both... Her position as a wife and as an equal individual.

Val sighed into her glass, then took another sip of the wine. Were the two facets irrevocably opposed? she wondered. Or was there a middle ground, where the best of both could not only meet but merge?

Yes, with the right man, Val decided. But was Jonas that man? Not the Jonas she knew. But could Jonas become that man? A tiny smile brushed Val's lips. Maybe, if she gently nudged him in the right direction. He'd resist, she knew that, but . . .

"Aren't you feeling well, Valerie?" The concerned sound of Marge's voice drew Val from her reverie. "You've barely touched your food."

"I'm fine," Val said. "I'm just not very hungry."

"Val's watching her weight, Marge," Jonas drawled, in an indulgent tone that surprised Val, until she recalled their pact for the evening.

"A bit too stringently, I'd say," Lynn interjected. "I can remember when Jonas preferred a more curvaceous woman." Her voice was silky, and the look she gave Jonas was blatantly suggestive. "Didn't you, darling?"

Val steeled herself for the twinge of jealousy she always experienced whenever Lynn made a remark designed to remind her of Jonas's previous attraction. The twinge didn't . . . twinge. Surprised, she looked at Jonas and murmured, "Really?"

"Yes, when I was young and green." His smile was sardonic. "My taste in women has improved with age and experience." Jonas raised his glass and tilted it at Val in a silent salute. "I'd say my taste has been refined, as well."

Flushed with pleasure, Val returned his salute. "Thank you, my love." She deliberately emphasized the endearment. "I'd say my taste is even more refined than yours."

"Love." Lynn's tone made the word sound dirty. She sneered at Jonas. "For you it's love of a pretty, fawning woman." Her glittering gaze shot to Val. "And for you it's love of money and position."

Val gasped, appalled by the woman's viciousness.

"Mother!" Mary Beth exclaimed in shock.

"Mon Dieu!" Jean-Paul exploded.

"That's enough, Lynn!" Marge ordered.

"The checkbook is closed." Jonas's frigid voice cut through the uproar.

Checkbook? Val frowned. Confused, she shifted her gaze to Lynn. The woman's stricken expression startled her. Val didn't understand. Since Jonas had obtained his divorce from Lynn on the grounds of desertion, he had not been required to pay her any alimony or support. Yet from what he had just said, it was obvious Jonas had been supporting Lynn on a voluntary basis, and his coldly stated decision to cease writing checks had shaken the woman considerably.

"Jonas, you wouldn't!" Lynn cried.

"You think not?" Jonas's eyes were as cold as his voice. "Watch me."

Val knew that expression. Jonas used it whenever he was dead set on a course of action. When Jonas said "Watch me" in that tone of voice, everyone around him searched for cover.

"But, Jonas," Lynn said. "What will I do for money? How will I live?"

Jonas had been supporting Lynn! Shock jolted through Val. All these years. She had never so much as suspected....

"You could go to work," Jonas suggested dryly.

The color drained from Lynn's face. "But I have no training! I could never earn enough—"

"To provide the luxuries my money has afforded you," he finished for her. Lynn turned pleading eyes to her daughter, but before she could utter a word, Jonas said, "And don't look to Mary Beth for support, because I'll stop her allowance and convince Jean-Paul to withhold his money."

Lynn's lovely mouth curled into an ugly twist, and she lashed out at him nastily, "You really are a bastard."

Val gasped and pushed back her chair. Jonas clasped her arm to hold her still.

"Sit down," he said to Mary Beth, who had cried out in protest and jumped to her feet.

"But, Dad . . ." she began.

Jonas gently cut her off. "It's all right, honey."

"It's not all right," Marge argued, glaring at Lynn.

"It's unforgivable," Jean-Paul muttered.

"It's true," Jonas said flatly.

"Jonas," Val murmured, sliding her palm over the back of his hand. Jonas didn't look at her, but continued to glare at Lynn.

"I'll sell the house in the South of France," Lynn threatened.

Jonas laughed in her face. "You really should pay closer attention to details, Lynn."

"What do you mean?" Lynn was looking scared again.

"The house in France isn't yours to sell." His smile was devoid of humor. "It never was."

The tension was palpable. In silence, everyone waited to hear Lynn's response.

Lynn glared down the length of the table at Jonas for several long, drawn-out seconds, then caved in. "I'll make a bargain with you, Jonas," she said in a strangled-sounding, subdued voice.

Jonas arched one eyebrow in mockery. "You're not in a position to bargain," he reminded her.

"Will you just listen?" Lynn pleaded.

Unmoved, Jonas continued to stare at her. The very air in the room seemed to stretch and quiver.

Mary Beth was the first to break. "Dad, please, listen to what she has to say!" she cried.

Still Jonas continued to observe his former wife with his hard, unyielding stare.

"Jonas," Val whispered, growing concerned at the paleness of his daughter's face.

At her murmur Jonas's eyes flickered, then he relented. "All right, Lynn, I'll hear you out." His tone was chilling. "But it'd better be good."

Lynn wet her lips, swallowed, then said in a rush, "If you'll continue with my allowance as before, I'll return to the South of France."

"Forever?"

"Jonas, I want to be with Mary Beth when the baby's due!" Lynn protested.

Jonas sneered. "A little late in the game for maternal instincts, isn't it?" He waved a hand to silence her when she started to object. "All right, Lynn. I'll maintain you in the life-style you've become accustomed to," he said.

Val had not taken her eyes off Jonas throughout the exchange. When the tension eased, she stole a glance at Lynn. This time she did feel a twinge of pity for the older woman. Failure, not only in this one instance, but the failure of an entire life lurked in the depths of Lynn's eyes. Lynn was vanquished, silenced.

Val suspected that Lynn would eventually regroup to strike again, but at least until Mary Beth's child arrived, her viperous tongue had been stilled.

To Val's relief, the remainder of the evening passed without further incident. Lynn excused herself and retired after the first of the belated toasts that were raised to the expectant couple. The natural soft pink color returned to Mary Beth's cheeks. Jean-Paul was amusing in his pride of accomplishment. Marge was obviously eager for her first great-grandchild. Even

Jonas managed to laugh, despite the evidence of anger still smoldering in his eyes.

Val was grateful that the party broke up early. She was exhausted and had a raging headache. The effort she was expending to keep up the pretense of being happy with Jonas was beginning to wear on her nerves.

At that moment, Val wasn't at all happy with Jonas. She had been hurt, deeply hurt by the discovery that he was supporting Lynn. But it wasn't the knowledge that he was making regular payments to Lynn that bothered Val. What Jonas did with his money was his business. No, what had wounded her was the realization that Jonas had not told her that he had been keeping Lynn for years.

And Val felt certain his failure to tell her had been deliberate, for it was obvious the other members of his family knew, including Jean-Paul.

What did his secrecy say about their marriage? Val asked herself, sitting stiff and unresponsive beside her husband in the car as they drove home. In her opinion, it certainly didn't indicate trust or openness or communication. And without those elements, a marriage wasn't a marriage at all. It was a sham, a farce, a convenience.... His.

In brooding silence, Val preceded Jonas into the house. Feeling humiliated, sick, used, she mounted the stairs. She didn't go to their bedroom. Ignoring the purposeful sound of his tread behind her, she went into the guest room and shut the door in his face. She had taken two steps into the room when the door rebounded off the wall.

"What the hell do you think you're doing?" Jonas demanded. Storming after her, he grasped her by the arm and spun her around to face him.

Though his hold wasn't painful, Val stared pointedly at his hand. When he released her, she raised her eyes to his. "I'm going to sleep here."

"You're still angry." It was not a question.

Val sighed. "No, Jonas, I'm not still angry. I'm angry again. Angry and hurt and—" she raised a hand to massage a throbbing temple "—and tired, so tired."

"Of me?" he asked tersely.

She lifted a hand, then let it fall to her side. "At this moment, yes. Of you, of everything." Her eyes were bright with tears she refused to let fall, her shoulders drooped. Defeat lay on her like an immense weight.

"This is about Lynn, isn't it?"

Val gave a short, humorless laugh. She knew by the sound of his voice, that arrogant note, that his back was up. If there was one thing Jonas detested, it was having his actions questioned. By anyone.

"You're angry because I've been supporting her," he persisted. "Aren't you?"

Val longed to curl up in a corner and weep. Instead she straightened her spine and lifted her small chin in defiance. "And shouldn't I be?"

Jonas reflected her action with the thrust of his hard jaw. "It's my money, Val. I earned it. And I'll do with it as I damn well please."

His tone broke the last thread of her composure. "I don't care about your damned money!" she shouted. "Give it away," she said wildly. "Throw it away. Burn it. I don't care!" Fighting to regain control, she spun away. A startled gasp burst from her throat when he grabbed her arm and swung her around once more to face the building anger in his eyes.

"Then what the hell is this all about?" he demanded. "What's biting at you?"

"Trust, Jonas!" Val said. "A solid marriage is built on trust. Yet you didn't trust me enough to tell me that you've been keeping Lynn all this time." She drew a quick harsh breath. "It was obvious that everyone else knew—Marge, Mary Beth, Jean-Paul, and God knows how many others."

"Val...I—" Jonas began, but she wasn't finished. Her voice cut across his.

"You've been keeping Lynn for years. And you've hidden it from me," she accused heatedly. "Exactly as you would keep a mistress."

"Mistress!" Jonas barked. "Is that what this is really about?" Grasping her by the shoulders, he shook her, not roughly, but as if trying to shake sense into her. "Damn it, Val, I wouldn't touch Lynn with a dirty stick, and you know it. Or at least you should. I love you, damn it!" he shouted. "And you should know that, too."

"You really don't understand, do you?" Weighed down by defeat, Val's body sagged, and was literally held erect by his strong hands.

"Understand what, for God's sake?"

"You don't love, you possess," she replied dully. "I'm *your* wife, *your* possession, your *thing*." Her voice grew thin. "Your woman." Shaking off his hands with her last bit of strength, Val moved away from him. "I'm very tired, Jonas," she said, turning to look at him. "If you don't mind . . ."

"I do mind." Though his voice revealed the strain and anger he was feeling, Jonas made no attempt to close the distance separating them. His frustration was evident by the way he raked his hand through his hair. "What do you want that I haven't given you, Val?"

"Full partnership," she answered at once.

"In the company?" Jonas looked genuinely confused.

"No, you blockhead!" Val retorted, stung by the very fact that he had thought immediately of his business. "I don't want half of your company. I want half of your personal life!" She laughed; the sound held a hint of encroaching hysteria. "Hell," she cried. "I'd be satisfied with the consideration you extend to your female executives!"

"Val, calm down." Jonas took a step toward her.

Val took two steps back and held up her hand. "Go away, Jonas." Her short, choppy words betrayed her crumbling inner resources. "It's late. I'm exhausted. I don't want to argue anymore."

"Val . . ." Jonas took another step.

Val broke completely. "Jonas, please!"

He hesitated, his expression stark with concern. "I don't want to leave you like this. Come with me," he coaxed, as if placating an overwrought child. "Come to bed with me. Let me hold you."

Because she was so very tired, and because, despite everything, she loved him so very much, Val was sorely tempted to chuck it all—all her needs as a woman, all her principles, all her ambitions for a true union with him—to give up and surrender to him. Jonas himself saved her by murmuring four inflammatory words.

"Let me love you."

A sad smile skipped over Val's mouth. "That's your answer, your cure-all for everything. Make love, and the problem will go away."

"No, but—" Jonas began.

Val silenced him with a sharp shake of her head. "Not this time, Jonas. I thought I made that clear last night."

"We need to talk, Val," he said adamantly.

"Yes." Val nodded. "But first we need to think, long and hard, about what we want as individuals. Because you see, Jonas, whether you approve or not, I *am* an individual. Not your shadow. Not your echo. But a real, live person. But for now I'm tired," she said, unconsciously echoing his words of the night before. "I'm going to bed."

Chapter Five

Estrangement. Jonas hated the word and all the pain that it entailed: becoming distant, unfriendly, the denial of feeling. Jonas hated it. Yet the word precisely described his relationship with Val.

Two weeks, he thought, kneading the tight muscles at the back of his neck. Almost two full weeks had elapsed since the night of Marge's celebration dinner.

Some celebration. The noise Jonas made sounded like a snort.

Pushing his chair away from his large, cluttered desk, he strode to the wide window of his office. It was late. It was dark. Artificial light illuminated the company parking lot, empty except for the small cluster of vehicles belonging to the office cleaning service and the night security personnel, and for his own car, parked directly beneath his office window, looking oddly abandoned.

Did Val's car look abandoned, sitting alone in the four-car garage attached to the house? Jonas wondered, sightlessly staring at the gleaming Lincoln six floors below.

No. Of course it didn't. Val's car wasn't even in the garage, Jonas thought derisively, turning back to his desk. Val wasn't at home, nor would she be, he recalled. It was Friday, the night before the wedding. Val had informed him that she'd be spending the entire night with Janet, doing whatever it was women did the night before a wedding.

Jonas smiled wryly as he settled into his chair. Considering her present attitude toward the institution, Val was probably trying to talk Janet into changing her mind about getting married, before it was too late.

Suddenly needing to hear Val's voice, even if it was the distant one she had used through every conversation of the previous two weeks, Jonas reached for the no-nonsense black console phone set close at hand at the right side of his desk. His fingers grasped the receiver, but he didn't pick it up. Exhaling impatiently, he drew back his hand.

He had work to do, and he wouldn't get it done chatting on the phone. The admonition to himself might have been funny under normal circumstances. Tonight it merely served to drive home the truth of the situation: he and his wife were barely speaking. The idea of the two of them chatting was ludicrous.

But then, had he and Val ever relaxed enough with each other to engage in a simple chat?

The thought made Jonas uncomfortable. Although he didn't like admitting it, he knew they had seldom shared a meaningful conversation, let alone a friendly chat. Feeling suddenly prickly all over, Jonas shifted in his chair, and was grateful for the distraction presented by the abrupt intrusion of his assistant, who entered the room without his usual polite knock.

"What are you doing here?" Jonas demanded. "Aren't you supposed to be out somewhere, getting drunk or something on your last night of freedom?"

Charlie McAndrew grinned at his employer. "The bachelor party was last week, remember?"

Jonas groaned. "How can I forget?" He motioned the younger man into a chair with a flick of his hand. "You have some wild friends, Charlie," he observed, remembering with distaste the drunken revelry the other men had indulged in the previous week. Jonas had never met any one of the five men before, all of whom had been college buddies of Charlie's. Jonas wasn't thrilled about spending the entire day with them tomorrow, either. "I can only hope they'll all be sober enough to seat the guests and stand up through the wedding ceremony."

Charlie dropped into the chair with a tired-sounding sigh and an even more tired-sounding excuse. "They don't get out alone all that often."

Jonas arched a skeptical brow. "Are they caged?"

"Close," Charlie replied with a laugh. "They are all very much married."

"Which you will be in less than twenty-four hours," Jonas reminded him. "Is that how you view the state of matrimony?" he asked with interest. "As being caged?"

"No, of course not!" Charlie exclaimed.

"There's no of course about it," Jonas said. "You'll be as very much married as they are," he pointed out reasonably. "Where's the difference?"

Instead of answering, Charlie responded with a question. "You're married. Do you feel caged?"

Though Jonas stiffened, he considered the question before giving a reply. Did he feel caged by marriage? Without looking, Jonas could see the plain gold band encircling the third finger of his left hand. Had he ever felt constricted by the binding band of metal? He slowly shook his head from side to side. Frustrated, yes, but... "No," Jonas answered both Charlie and himself.

"And there's the difference." Charlie shrugged.

Jonas frowned. "You lost me."

"It's the woman," Charlie explained. "Brad's married to a grind, and he hears nothing but nag, nag, nag. Ted's wife is a spender. She wants everything yesterday. George's wife is house-proud, makes him go outside to smoke his pipe. Jeff's wife is cold, and starves him for sexual warmth. And Randy's wife is a clinging vine, which bolstered his ego at the beginning, but is strangling him now."

Jonas frowned in disapproval. "They discuss their marital problems with you and each other?"

"We've all been friends for a long time, Jonas. I don't know—" he shrugged "—I guess it helps to talk about it. Maybe it's either that or explode."

"Maybe." Jonas didn't sound convinced. "But don't you think they'd be better advised to talk about it with their wives, rather than each other?"

"Sure," Charlie agreed. "But I gather that they have tried that and failed. In any case, do you understand what I mean about the difference being in the woman?" he asked. "You and I are the lucky ones. We both found exceptional women."

Jonas thought about the conversation long after he had thrown Charlie out of the office with a growled order to go home and get some rest.

In what way were Val and Janet exceptional? he mused, once again wandering to the wide window. With respect to Janet, the answer was simple. She was exceptionally bright, exceptionally talented, exceptionally well-balanced and even-tempered. Jonas felt certain Janet would make a terrific wife for the ambitious, yet basically shy Charlie...or any other man.

But Val? In what way was his wife exceptional? Jonas frowned, and recalled the complaints of Charlie's friends. Val was certainly not a shrew. She never nagged him about anything. She wasn't a spender, either, even though he had given her several credit cards and had set up a large household account for her at his bank. She didn't cling like a smothering vine and, thank heaven, Val was definitely not cold in bed.

At least, she hadn't been cold while she was still sharing his bed. A deep sigh was wrenched from his throat. Hearing the longing underlying his sigh, Jonas dragged his attention back to the subject under consideration.

In what way was Val exceptional and different from all the other women he had known? In many ways, Jonas acknowledged. Then he laughed, softly. Hell, the Val of today was even more different and more exceptional than the Val he had first come to know over three years ago.

Casting his mind back in time, Jonas recalled her as she had been when they'd met. She'd had an elusive, wistful look. Her fantastic violet eyes had revealed the grief she was still suffering from after the tragic death of her fiancé just two weeks before their scheduled wedding day. She had an uninterested look, as if she no longer cared what happened to her. She had been breathtakingly beautiful, soft and extremely vulnerable, and instilled in most men the urge to care for and protect.

But her vulnerability hadn't been the snare that had captured Jonas's interest. He had worked too hard, had come too far on his journey from bastard orphan to the owner of one of the largest electronics firms in the world, to be moved to anything other than impatience with her vulnerability. Jonas had no time for anyone, male or female, who retired from the battlefield of life. No, what had initially caught his attention and interest was the spark of angry defiance Val had shown during their very first verbal exchange. Within hours, his interest had changed to desire, and within the few weeks she had worked as his private secretary, that desire had expanded to fill his waking and sleeping hours.

Jonas could remember how he'd wanted her as if it were yesterday. He had stood at this same window, his muscles aching, his body taut, his mind centered on one thought.

God, he wanted her.

He still did.

Feeling his body tighten in response to his memories, Jonas turned away from the window and forced his thought into safer channels.

Yes, the Val of today was vastly different from the woman he had met three years ago. Although she was still breathtakingly beautiful—no, more so—still soft, still gentle, her spark of defiance had blossomed into a determination that nearly equaled his own.

I am not a thing.

The echo of Val's voice whispered through his mind. His anger flaring anew, Jonas strode to the door, past the work he had planned on finishing that evening. The work would still be waiting for him when he returned.

Val was not waiting for him. The house was dark when he got home. Dark and empty. It seemed too big, too spacious without Val's presence to lend welcoming warmth.

Trailing through to the kitchen, Jonas opened the refrigerator, looking for something to appease his protesting, empty stomach. As usual he had skipped lunch. A covered baking dish sat at the front of the center shelf. Jonas was reaching for the casserole when the phone rang. Leaving the refrigerator door open, he crossed to the kitchen phone.

"Thorne," he said into the receiver, in exactly the same way he answered his office phone.

"Surprise, surprise," Val drawled, causing the emptiness inside Jonas to expand into aching need. "Have you found your dinner?" she went on to ask.

Jonas shot a glance at the open refrigerator and casserole on the center shelf. "I think so. The baking dish?"

"The same," Val said in a dry tone.

"What is it?" Jonas really didn't care; he just wanted to keep her talking.

"Macaroni and ham casserole."

"What do I do with it?"

Val's impatient sigh sang along the line to him. "You heat it in the microwave and eat it, Jonas."

"I know that," he retorted. "But you know I never use the micro, Val. What setting do I use?"

"You're the electronic wizard," Val said sweetly. "You figure it out." With that, she hung up.

Naturally, Jonas did figure it out. It required thirty seconds of his time to read the instruction manual that came with the appliance. The steam rising from the bubbling mixture of macaroni and chunks of ham smothered in a creamy cheese sauce sharpened his appetite when he removed the dish from the microwave a few minutes later.

Jonas ate his dinner perched on a stool at the breakfast counter. Under normal conditions he would have relished the food. Tonight he simply ate it to appease the hungry growl of his stomach. But then he wasn't dining under normal conditions, he reminded himself.

As if he needed reminding, Jonas thought, staring at the phone. He wanted to talk to Val. Not true. He wanted to see her. Wrong. What Jonas really wanted was to hold her, love her, never let her go.

With one emptiness filled, the deeper emptiness was fully exposed. It had been exactly two full weeks since Jonas had held Valerie in his arms, kissed her with his mouth, loved her with his body. Two weeks of stilted conversation, meaningless words, thick, heavy constraint. How he had longed to break through the cloak of reserve Val had drawn around herself, her emotions, he reflected, automatically scraping and rinsing the dishes before stacking them in the dishwasher.

As he returned the untouched portion of the meal to the refrigerator, a consideration struck Jonas. It was strange, but although Val was barely speaking to him, she continued to keep the house spotless, do the laundry and grocery shopping, and cook for him, not just any old thrown-together meals, but some of his favorites.

Val confused him, and Jonas didn't appreciate the feeling. He had never understood her adamant refusal to have help in the house, other than the woman who came in once a month to do the heavy cleaning. He was a wealthy man; he could easily afford to have live-in help for Val. Yet she insisted on doing it all, or the majority of it, herself, claiming that since Jonas rarely entertained on a lavish scale, she didn't require or want additional help.

Shaking his head, Jonas wandered through the empty house and up the stairs. A sigh whispered from his throat as he passed the closed door to the guest room.

After a quick shower, Jonas grimaced and slid between the freshly laundered sheets. He didn't appreciate the sudden emptiness of the king-size bed any more than he valued his state of confusion. And he knew that if Val went through with her plans to fly to the West Coast at the end of the coming week, the house, the bed and he himself would feel not only empty, but deserted as well.

Why was Val being so damn stubborn? Jonas railed in silent frustration. What did she want or expect from him? Damn it, he was faithful to her and honest with her. He had happily provided for her not only the necessities, but luxuries beyond the wildest imaginings of many other women. And he loved her to the marrow of his bones. What more could he offer her? Why was she so restless and dissatisfied with their life together? Even as Jonas asked the silent question, the memory of their bitter argument tormented his tired mind.

Trust. Val had accused him of not according her the trust necessary to a successful marriage.

But he did trust Val, Jonas defended himself. It was other men he didn't trust. And in the sorry case of Lynn, Jonas had believed he was right in keeping the fact that he was supporting Lynn to himself. It had nothing to do with Val. Well, at least the question of Lynn was now resolved. With her usual flair for the dramatic, Lynn had departed Philadelphia for France the previous Monday.

Partnership. Val had insisted upon being a complete and equal part of his life.

But didn't she know how very much a part of his life she was? Jonas wondered. *Equal?* Hell, she *was* his life. Didn't she know that? Then again, how could she know? he mused. When was the last time they'd talked, not just about trivial matters, but really talked to each other? When had they ever communicated, understood, touched base intellectually and emotionally?

Jonas shifted beneath the light weight of the smooth sheet. He had been too busy with the company, he excused himself—or attempted to. There had never been enough time. Three years of being too busy and not having enough time? Jonas jeered at himself. And through every one of those too busy years without enough time he had refused her pleas to return to work. She was his wife. And Jonas Thorne's wife did not work outside the home.

His wife.

His possession.

His woman.

Jonas winced. Was it any wonder Val had attempted to fill the lonely hours of her days with courses and causes? And had he, in his superior wisdom, understood, or better yet, encouraged Val in her quest for fulfillment?

Not he, Jonas derided himself. Not the electronic genius. Not the strong, fiercely independent and individualistic man who had fought his way from the stigma of bastard and the brutality of a foster home to a position of wealth and respect. No, instead of helping his wife realize her full potential as a woman, he had demanded she stay home and play house.

When had he stopped thinking in matters concerning Val?

When had he ever started?

Rolling onto his back, Jonas stared into the middle distance. He knew the answer to his own question. He had never done any rational thinking about Val, simply because his emotions always got in the way.

Val had told him that they both needed to do some thinking about their relationship. She had been thinking about it for two weeks at least, and very probably much longer. It had taken him nearly two weeks to work his way up to thinking about it. She had said that when they were finished thinking, they'd talk. Jonas was ready to talk now.

Flinging back the sheet, he sat up and reached for the phone. His hand fell away before it touched the plastic receiver. He couldn't force the issue, couldn't take the chance of having her accusing him of once again trying to assert his will over her. He had no other option than to wait until she was ready.

I am an individual.

The echo of Val's voice whispered through his mind. And though Jonas was aching for her, longing to go after her, bring her home and enclose her in his arms forever, he contented himself with sending her a silent reply.

In spades, sweetheart.

While Jonas had his mind full of questions, Val had her hands full trying to keep the nervous bride calm.

"Oh, God, am I doing the right thing?" Janet wailed, pacing up and down her living room.

"Yes, Janet," Val said in a soothing tone.

"But I'm nearly forty years old!"

"What does that have to do with anything?"

Janet came to an abrupt halt at the low coffee table, picked up her glass and took a sip of champagne Valerie had brought with her. "Nothing, I suppose," she mumbled into the glass. When she looked at Val there was fear in her eyes. "Do you think I'm too old to have a child?"

Val was taken aback. "Are you pregnant?"

"No!" Janet exclaimed. Then, more quietly, "No, I'm not pregnant. But suppose I should get pregnant. What then?"

"You'll have a baby?" Val asked in wide-eyed innocence.

Janet frowned. Then she laughed. "I'm acting rather silly, aren't I?"

Val smiled. "You're acting like a bride on the eve of her big day."

"You didn't get crazy the night before your wedding," Janet pointed out. And, since Val had stayed with her at the time, Janet was in a position to know.

"Yes, well," Val murmured, "Jonas didn't give me time to get really crazy. You've had months of planning and preparation to help you along," she said, hoping to divert Janet from the topic of Jonas. Her ploy failed.

"No, Jonas didn't give you much time," Janet said, her tone full of musing remembrance. "About two weeks, wasn't it?"

"Mmm." Val nodded, concealing a wince behind the glass she raised to her lips.

"It seems so long ago now."

Val arched her eyebrows.

"I mean, it seems now that you and Jonas have been together forever," Janet explained.

"Does it?" Val asked vaguely, thinking that the past two weeks had seemed like forever.

"Yes," Janet replied, taking off again, this time in the direction of the kitchen. "I've got to get something to eat. I'm famished."

"Nerves," Val said with authority.

"Do you want something?"

"Yes." Standing, Val carried her glass into the kitchen, thinking that she had nerves to feed herself.

Tears trickled down Val's face. She didn't try to check the flow. After months of frantic activity, and the morning's confusion of getting dressed, then to the church with a bride and six attendants, all with nerves on the brink of twanging out of control, the procession went off like clockwork. The solemn ceremony was touching in its beauty and serenity.

Val's tears were for the lovely bride and the endearingly attractive bridegroom, to be sure, but mostly for the devastatingly handsome best man.

Jonas.

As she preceded Janet down the aisle, Val's heart had contracted at the sight of him, standing tall and composed at Charlie's right side. The wedding guests packing the church faded as her vision focused on Jonas's imposing form. Her steps correctly measured, Val closed the distance between them. Then he was momentarily lost to her sight as she stepped to the left and turned to watch Janet take the remaining steps to her bridegroom's side.

Her tears began to fall halfway through the ceremony. Under cover of the cascading bouquet she carried, Val rubbed her thumb over her marriage rings. The words of the service were muted by her thoughts.

How very different this service was from the one that had united her with Jonas. Valerie had had a similar thought on the day Mary Beth and Jean-Paul were married. Val had not had the round of showers and parties both Janet and Mary Beth had been treated to. She had not had the excitement and the hassles of fittings and shopping and last-minute details to be seen to, either. Val had not been decked out like a fairy princess in yards and yards of China silk and imported lace, as Mary Beth had been. Nor had she been dressed in skillfully cut shimmering satin, as Janet now was.

With the clarity of her inner eye, Val could see the suit she'd worn for the occasion. It was nice, but not spectacular. Jonas had not worn a tuxedo. He had been attired in a three-piece suit, attractive, but not special. They had not been married in a church. There had not been a note of music. They had recited their vows before a judge in his chambers.

Yet Valerie had never felt any less married than any other woman.

And now, standing beside her friend, two bodies away from her husband, Valerie ached with the need to touch the man she had married under such inauspicious, mundane circumstances.

Two weeks. It seemed like forever.

She came into his arms in a swirling cloud of warm satin and heady perfume.

Lord, she was beautiful, Jonas thought, his pulse quickening as he enfolded Val in his arms for the wedding party dance. She looked good. She smelled good. She felt ... wonderful.

Jonas and Valerie had not danced together very often over the past three years, yet they moved as one, in perfect timing to the haunting music of a current love song.

"I missed you last night." Jonas startled himself with the unplanned, open admission. The surprise in the eyes Val raised to his indicated he had startled her also.

"Did you?" Her tone indicated that though she was startled, she was equally skeptical.

"Of course I did," Jonas said in an impatient whisper. "The house felt empty."

Val met his impatience with cool reserve. "I'm well acquainted with the feeling."

Her shot hit home. Ignoring the hint of warning, Jonas persisted. "It's going to feel even emptier after you leave for California next week."

"I'll only be away for four days, Jonas," Val reminded him. "You've often been away twice as long."

"That was business," Jonas said defensively.

"I know." Val smiled at the couple dancing by. "The house was just as empty. I was just as alone."

"Val..."

The music ended. Val danced out of his arms.

Had he heard what she'd said? Had he understood? Val's thinking process was unaffected by the male arms that had caught her as she spun away from Jonas. The arms belonged to Ted, one of Charlie's friends and groomsmen. He was a pleasant enough young man, good-looking and well built. But when compared to Jonas, he paled into insignificance.

Had he heard a word she'd said? Did he give a damn? Val gave the large reception hall of the country club a casual scan, her eyes searching for the tall, imposing figure of her husband. She spotted Jonas at the edge of the dance floor, conversing with a plump, matronly woman, whom Val recognized as the wife of an important business associate of his.

Business. Val smothered a sigh, and smiled at whatever it was Ted had said to her. With Jonas it was always business. Val didn't actually resent Jonas's devotion to his company. She understood the force of the ambition that drove him. He was a self-made man. Jonas was on top in his particular field and fully intended to remain there.

But there were times, more and more frequent in number, when she wished Jonas would delegate more and work less. He had not taken a vacation, a real getaway vacation, since she'd met him. They spent very little "quality time" together. They had never played together with the abandonment of other couples, married or single, on a carefree holiday. The work was a joy to him, Val knew. She also knew that his work was a growing strain on their relationship. If only...

The music ended. Val murmured the appropriate inanities, then turned toward the spot where she had last seen Jonas. He wasn't there. Wandering aimlessly around the room, her restless gaze skimming the faces of some of the over three hundred guests, Val stalked her husband.

She eventually found him leaning against a decorative Grecian pillar while he observed the gathering with an aloof, contemplative expression. He'd been watching her progress, and his eyes narrowed as she approached him.

"You're the best man," Val reminded him as she came to a stop in front of him.

"I know." Jonas smiled.

Val chose to ignore his wry humor. "You should be mingling with the guests." She knew what was coming when his smile grew.

"If I'm going to mingle, sweetheart, I'll..."

"Jonas." Val silenced him with that single warning murmur. "This is hardly the time or the place."

Supremely unconcerned with the laughter and conversation rippling around them, Jonas rooted her to the floor with an intense stare. "When is the time?" he asked softly. "Where is the place?

The room was suddenly too warm. Val's gown was suddenly too tight across her breasts. She couldn't think. She didn't want to. In that instant, all the discord between them dissolved in the achingly familiar heat that was rushing to her head, plunging to the depths of her femininity. Val was unaware that her feelings were clearly revealed in her violet eyes. All she knew was that she longed to drown in the blue-gray depths of his eyes.

Normally a man of few words, Jonas didn't speak; he acted. Pushing away from the ornate pillar, he grasped her hand and led her around the fringes of the crowd and through the open doors that led to the spacious patio and extensive country club gardens.

The intoxicating scent of roses permeated the soft summer air. The velvet night sky sparkled with the light of millions of stars and the nearly full moon. A thrilling sensation of strangely illicit excitement trembled through Val's overwarm body.

She came to her senses when Jonas came to a stop, midway along one of the graveled walkways. Val had to smile at the first coherent thought that swam into her head. She was literally being led down the garden path. The low, terse sound of his voice jolted her back to reality.

"When are you coming home?"

"I was only away one night, Jonas."

Jonas released his grasp on her hand and then, catching her off guard, pulled her into his arms. His voice was a low, hungry growl near her ear. "I mean, when are you really coming home, back to our bed, where you belong?"

Resistance flowed along Val's spine. Always the same, she thought. It was always the same. For Jonas, the cure to any personal problem could be found in bed. Working a hand free, she pressed it against his shoulder.

"Jonas, don't."

"Don't?" he repeated in an incredulous tone. "Val, I need you so much I can hardly think straight." Sliding a hand up her spine to her nape, he tangled his fingers in her hair and tugged her head back, "And you tell me 'Don't'? You might as well tell me to stop breathing." Lowering his head, he fastened his mouth onto hers.

His kiss was heaven. His kiss was hell. And it was all the levels of sensation quivering between the two extremes. It was always the same . . . yet always different. His mouth was hard, yet warm. His lips were demanding, yet tender. His tongue was piercing, yet gentle.

Needing the feel of Jonas, the taste of him, every bit as much as his taut body told her that he needed her, Val stole a moment out of their time of discord and surrendered to the sweet forgetfulness of his kiss.

Her spine bowed in response to the tightening of his arm around her waist. Her soft, trembling body was fused to the rigid strength of his. Plundering her mouth, Jonas arched protectively, possessively, over her slight form.

Her gown was being crushed; Valerie didn't care. The curve of her spine was being strained; Valerie didn't feel it. For the length of his kiss, her mind abdicated, her senses rejoiced, her passion reigned.

His breath was a harsh sound on the still night when Jonas lifted his mouth from hers. "You want me as much as I want you." His voice was low, raspy, intense. "Come home with me, Val. Come home and make love with me."

With the despairing thought that lovely dreams always seemed to end in rude awakenings, Val brought her hand from his shoulder and laid her palm against his cheek.

Disarmed and heartened, Jonas combed his fingers through the silky strands of her hair, gleaming ebony in the wash of moonlight, and eased his grip around her waist. "Val," he murmured, lowering his head for another kiss.

Her small hand stroked his cheek, then she nimbly slipped out of his loosened embrace. "It would solve nothing, Jonas," she said from a safe distance of several feet. "Except to alleviate the obvious, immediate discomfort."

Stiff with anger and frustration, Jonas cursed under his breath. Watching him warily, prepared to make a run for it if he took one step toward her, Val listened to him swear in mounting surprise, amazed at his extensive vocabulary.

When he at last fell silent, after having not once used the same word twice, Val asked, "Are you quite finished?"

Jonas had the grace to be embarrassed. "I'm sorry," he said, raking a hand through his neatly brushed hair. "But you have a positive talent for making me mad."

"That's my line," Val quipped, in a weak attempt to defuse his explosive temper.

His burst of laughter was harsh, short, involuntary. But it did the trick. Jonas exhaled, easing the stiffness from his body. "And you've been using it a lot lately." He took a step toward her; Val took a step back. In the bright moonlight she could see the cynical smile that curved his thin lips. "You can relax, sweetheart," he said, slowly moving toward her. "I won't pounce on you again."

Ignoring the twinge of disappointment she felt, Val gave him a considering look. "I'd like your word on it."

"You have it."

Val relaxed, and unwittingly offered him the compliment of physically displaying utter belief and trust in his given word. His smile tearing her poise into ribbons of shivering expectancy, Jonas closed the space that separated them.

"We must go back inside," Val said, clenching her hands into fists to combat the effects of his nearness on her senses. "As the best man and matron of honor, we are expected to mingle and be charming to the guests."

"I want to kiss you again."

"No, Jonas." Now she was denying herself as well as him.

"Just once more," he murmured seductively.

"No, Jonas." Refusing him hurt her.

"You're my wife."

Val lifted her chin. "Are you issuing a veiled ultimatum?" she challenged.

Jonas pinned her for an instant with an angry stare. Then he shook his head in sharp denial. "You know better."

Relief shivered through Val, for, although she thought Jonas would never force an issue with her, she wasn't absolutely sure. "Then I suggest we go back inside. In case you've forgotten, our friends are celebrating their wedding." Displaying a confidence she was light-years from feeling, Val turned and began walking toward the lights and sounds of music and laughter that were pouring from the open doors of the country club.

"I haven't forgotten a thing, Val," Jonas muttered, falling into step beside her.

You never do, Val acknowledged, but only to herself. To him she raised one delicately arched eyebrow. "Do we present a show of unity or dissension?" Her nod indicated the building they were approaching and the people inside.

"Unity." Marginally smiling, Jonas angled his arm in invitation.

Faintly returning his smile, Val slid her arm through his. She glanced up at him in startled surprise when he came to a halt mere inches from the open doors. "Jonas?"

"This is ridiculous." His tone was adamant. "We don't have time for socializing, Val. We must talk."

"Not here, Jonas." Her tone betrayed her impatience. It succeeded in igniting his own.

"When?" he demanded. He shouldn't have.

"When I return from California," she answered in a fierce whisper as they crossed the threshold. The arm beneath her hand grew taut, revealing the control Jonas was exerting over his temper.

"What?" Impervious to the startled looks sent their way from the guests who had overheard him, Jonas stared at her in furious disbelief.

Smiling sweetly for the benefit of the onlookers, Val repeated her answer, but this time succinctly and through her sparkling, gritted teeth. "I said when I get back from California, Jonas."

GIVE YOUR HEART TO SILHOUETTE®

FREE!

Mail this heart today!

Limited Time Offer! *Make sure you get this great FREE OFFER- act today!*

If offer card is missing, write to:
Silhouette Reader Service, P.O. Box 609, Fort Erie, Ontario L2A 5X3.

CLIP AND MAIL THIS POSTPAID CARD TODAY!

Business Reply Mail

No Postage Stamp Necessary if Mailed in Canada

Postage will be paid by

Silhouette Books®
P.O. Box 609
Fort Erie, Ontario
L2A 9Z9

Canada Post
Postes Canada

125

Chapter Six

The weather in San Francisco was miserable. It had rained, at times in pouring sheets, at others in light drizzles, throughout every one of the seemingly endless four days Val had been on the West Coast.

Val's mood was in perfect harmony with the prevailing weather conditions. The rally for the protection of artistic individuality, over which she had fought with Jonas to attend, was, at least for Val, a complete farce.

Bright-eyed and eager, Val had set out the morning after her arrival in San Francisco to be a part of the opening event. Disillusionment had set in minutes after she entered the designated display room.

The garish, childishly executed paintings on the sitting-room walls in the elegant home of one of the rally sponsors had nothing whatever to do with individuality, and even less with artistry. In Val's opinion, the general public deserved protection from the crude, overbearing idiot who had the temerity to refer to himself as a working artist.

Nevertheless, reserving judgment, Val sought out the sponsors she had corresponded with. They were not difficult to identify. Never before in her life had she encountered such a group of dilettantes, sycophants, pseudointellectuals and just plain phonies.

Edging away from the group, she unobtrusively drifted toward the front door. Slipping out of the house, Val went sightseeing in the rain.

When she got back to the hotel late in the afternoon of that first day, Val considered returning home. She felt foolish for making the trip in the first place. She was discouraged and depressed. Not even sightseeing in the city she had longed to explore had managed to lift her spirits.

And, irascible as he often was, Val missed Jonas even more than she had three years before, when she'd left him, ostensibly to visit her mother in Australia, but with every intention of not returning. After only one day away, Val ached for the sight of Jonas. Yet she knew that if she went home, she would have to explain to him why she had cut short the trip. There was no way she could lie to him about it. And, though Jonas might not say "I told you so," Val knew he would definitely think it. Unwilling to admit he'd been right, Val decided to remain in California.

During the remaining three days of her stay, Val followed the same routine. After breakfast, she made her way to the first scheduled rally event of the day, each of which grew successively worse. Then, having put in an appearance, she escaped to spend the day on her own.

By the end of the third day, Val concluded that being on her own, even in a city as interesting and varied as San Francisco, was not her idea of a fun time. If only she and Jonas had resolved their differences...

But they hadn't. Trudging along the sidewalks, all of which seemed either straight up or straight down, Val chastised herself for the aloof, withdrawn attitude she'd maintained with Jonas during the week between the wedding and her departure for the coast.

And all because of stupid pride...hers as well as his, Val acknowledged. But, stupid or not, Val's pride had still been smarting over the revelation that Jonas had been supporting Lynn financially. And Val knew that she had stung Jonas's pride by rejecting his advances the night of Janet and Charlie's wedding.

By spiriting her away from the reception, Jonas had initially excited, then angered Val. The setting of a moon-washed garden drenched with the heady scent of early summer roses had been conducive to romance. Jonas had not only ruined the mood with his blatant sexual overtures, he had thrown away the perfect opportunity to effect a reconciliation.

Why were married men so incredibly dense? Val railed in silent frustration, panting as she climbed yet another steep hill. She had often heard married men deride women, married as well as single, for being gullible enough to fall for a smooth line pitched by a glib-tongued male. Whenever she had overheard remarks of that nature, Val had had to bite back the urge to upbraid the speaker for his own lack of insight. Why, she'd asked herself, couldn't the poor fools—Jonas included—figure out that, if they gave even half as much attention to their wives or lady friends as they paid to their work, the glib-tongued men would be out of business?

And so, since Jonas had made Val angry by wasting the romantic setting of the garden, she had determined to let him cool his heels, waiting for the "talk" he'd insisted upon, until after she had returned from the coast.

There was one final event for her to attend—a large formal gala, to be held in the ballroom of one of the oldest, most prestigious hotels in the city. Val wasn't looking forward to the event, but since she had shelled out a bundle for two tickets in the vain hope that Jonas would condescend to join her, she was determined on going, alone or not…maybe because, though she was on her own, she was never completely alone.

Sitting in a cable car as it screeched down the paved face of a hill, Jonas was with her.

Wandering in and out of the stalls on Fisherman's Wharf, examining the ordinary and the exotic merchandise proffered there, Jonas was with her.

Standing on the bay shore, the wind whipping her hair around her head, watching the fog shroud the Golden Gate Bridge and the island of Alcatraz, Jonas was with her.

And as she dressed for the gala in the gown Jonas had so violently disapproved of, he was definitely with her, scowling in spirit, if not in person.

For three days after Val's departure for California, the employees of J.T. Electronics took great care to avoid their employer. To put it in their words: the cracker was on the warpath. In fact, Jonas was mad.

He was mad at the world, he was mad at Val, but most of all he was mad at himself. Being human and male, Jonas didn't like facing his own failings. But he had failed, and knew it. He had failed Val and, in so doing, had ultimately failed himself.

Frustrated, agitated, impatient, Jonas prowled the confines of his office just as he had three years previously, the first time Val had left him alone.

He and Val had been estranged then, too, Jonas recalled with painful clarity.

Come to that, Val had withdrawn from him at that time, too, in much the same way she'd withdrawn into herself after the wedding reception for Janet and Charlie.

Jonas came to a halt at his brooding spot before the wide window that overlooked the rear parking lot. A derisive smile curved his thin lips. He had spent an inordinate amount of time on this spot during the past three days, he reflected, fighting an inner battle with himself—one that he'd been waging in silence throughout every one of those three days.

Three years ago, Jonas had allowed Valerie a month. Now she had told him she would be gone four days.

Jonas made a rude sound. His assistant was off on a romantic honeymoon with one of his executives. Charlie and Janet were very likely making love at that very minute, Jonas thought with envy, while he, the boss, stood like a statue, staring out a window, aching in every inch of his being for his woman.

It's only two nights and one more day, Jonas told himself, staring bleakly at the golden glow of the sunset. He could wait one more day.

"Like hell."

Fully aware of growling the decision aloud, Jonas turned away from the window and strode to his desk. Stabbing the intercom with his long index finger, Jonas issued terse instructions to his secretary.

"Linda, I want the Lear made ready to depart for San Francisco tomorrow morning. Take care of it."

"At once, Jonas."

Even in this edgy mood, Jonas had to smile, if faintly, at the woman's immediate response. Linda wasn't a good secretary, she was damn near perfect. And at thirty-two she wasn't merely attractive, she was gorgeous.

When Jonas thought about it, which wasn't often, he invariably smiled. Linda had been handpicked and scrupulously trained by his former secretary, his wife, Valerie. If nothing else, Linda's presence in the outer office bespoke Val's trust in him.

It was something. Jonas hung on to that something like an invisible talisman.

The elegantly appointed hotel ballroom was packed. Tuxedoed men and exquisitely gowned and bejeweled women stood in small groups conversing with the cadre of "artists" for whom the benefit was being held.

If nothing else, the normally scruffy self-declared artists had cleaned up well, Val thought wryly as she drifted from one group to another. Even the obnoxious young man she'd had the misfortune to meet at the first day's event looked reasonably presentable, having made the supreme sacrifice of trimming his shaggy beard and having his too long, lank hair shampooed.

Quiet, composed, reserved, Valerie chose to sit at a table near the back of the room for dinner. The food was excellent. Val barely tasted it. The speeches were blessedly short. Val didn't hear them. Behind a façade of interest, she asked herself what in hell she was doing there, allowing herself to be bored to numbness, when she could be at home, fighting with her blockhead of a husband.

Steeped in her loneliness for the only man who possessed the power to make her pulse race and her heartbeat play leapfrog with itself, Val was immune to the blatantly overt looks sent her way by many of the men present.

When the dinner was at last concluded, Val followed the lead of the other guests and mingled, listening to bits of a discussion here, adding her voice to bits of conversation there, then moving on, restless, yet unwilling to return to her hotel room to be alone with her own thoughts and fears.

In her preoccupation, Val was as unaware of the speculative glances sweeping her face and form as she was of the impact of her appearance and the challenge presented by her cool, untouchable attitude.

She was repeatedly invited onto the dance floor. She politely, but repeatedly declined.

The evening dragged on. Beginning to wonder if the interminable reception would ever come to an end, Val was standing with a small group of women, sipping at a glass of champagne she really didn't want, when her wandering attention was snared by the throaty low exclamation made by the beautiful, thirtyish, self-admittedly bored woman standing beside her.

"Oh, my! Yes," the woman murmured. "Please, Santa, bring me that for Christmas!"

"I beg your pardon?" Val responded, frowning at the staring, avaricious expression on her companion's face.

"Him," the woman said, nodding to indicate someone behind Val. "I'll take him as is, no gift wrap necessary."

A chorus of avid agreement was raised by the other women in the group, all of whom had their glittering eyes glued to the person in question.

Mildly curious, and grateful for the interruption of the rather dull discussion, Val turned to see the paragon who had called forth a sheen of pure lust on the other women's faces. A spasm of shock quaked through her at the sight that met her eyes.

He was attired in an expertly tailored tuxedo that molded and defined his broad shoulders and long, rawboned frame. A knife-pleated, sparkling white shirt gave sharp contrast to the unrelieved black. His chiseled jaw held at an arrogant angle, spine straight, shoulders squared, the man stood framed in the wide ballroom doorway, his narrow-eyed gaze slowly taking inventory of the guests, who were staring at him in gaping curiosity.

"Who is he?" The awed question came from a gaunt middle-aged woman directly opposite Valerie.

"I don't know," the woman who had first spotted him responded in a husky, thought-revealing tone. "But I intend to find out."

Turning her back on the unexpected late arrival, Val took a sip of her wine, then said casually, "His name is Jonas Thorne."

"He looks important," one woman observed.

"He looks powerful," another woman opined.

"He looks like he'd be great in bed," the woman who'd first noticed him said bluntly.

Valerie concealed a smile behind the glass she raised to her lips. She had been through a scene like this before. At that time, the obvious sexual interest in Jonas revealed by other women had both shocked and dismayed her. After three years, all Val experienced was amusement and pity.

"I understand that he's married to a very possessive, jealous woman," she murmured.

"Aren't the terrific-looking ones always married?" the gaunt woman wailed.

"It's the story of my life." The other woman sighed.

"He may be married, but he's alone now," the original speaker noted in a tone of sheer calculation. "And," she continued, smiling with smug satisfaction, "he's heading my way."

Val nearly choked over the woman's capacity for self-deception. Besides herself, there were three women in the group, yet this one was convinced she had snared his attention. Refusing to turn, Val sipped her wine and waited. She knew when he came to a stop beside her; a thrill trickled along her spine.

"Valerie." His voice was low, controlled, sexy.

Val could actually feel the collective shudder of response that swept through her companions. Tilting her head, she gave him a distant smile. "Jonas. Let me introduce you to a few of the patrons of the rally." Val felt grateful for her excellent memory as she rattled off their names.

"Ladies," he said smoothly, inclining his head.

"Ladies," Val echoed, her tone dry, "I'd like you to meet my husband, Jonas Thorne."

"Cute." Jonas made the observation from the corner of the limousine. "When did you decide you enjoyed creating uncomfortable little scenes?" he asked, referring to the gasps of surprise Val had drawn from the women by introducing him as her husband, and the furious spate of questions that had followed, which he had saved her from enduring by whisking her from the ballroom. Before Val had a chance to interpret his actions, he had swept her from the hotel and into the long gray car.

Val shrugged. "I couldn't resist," she defended herself. "Those female barracudas were sizing you up like a side of beef on the auction block."

"And that bothered you?"

Since his voice was free of inflection, and his face was shadowed so that she couldn't read his expression, Val couldn't tell whether Jonas was pleased or annoyed. Nervous, but determined not to let him see it, she carefully kept her own tone bland. "As a member of their sex, their behavior demeaned me." She casually glanced out the side window and drew in a deep, calming breath. "May I ask where you're taking me?" she inquired as she turned back to him.

"My hotel."

Val felt a quick flash of irritation. "I have my own room, Jonas," she said grittily.

"I have an entire suite, Valerie," Jonas retorted.

"But my clothes are in my room!"

"Give me your key," he said, holding out his hand, palm up. "I'll send the driver to collect your things."

"But..."

Jonas's control snapped. "Damn it, Val, you're my wife! And though we've been sleeping in separate beds, I'll be damned if I'll tolerate sleeping in separate hotels." He paused to draw an exasperated-sounding breath. "I know the driver. He'll be careful packing your things...."

"I packed nearly everything this afternoon," Val informed him.

Jonas's shrug was a blur of movement in the shadows. "So, no big deal. He'll finish the packing, then deliver your cases to my hotel." His tone took on an edge of steel. "Now, give me your key...please."

Although his outburst had ignited Val's anger, she subsided and flipped the catch on her evening bag. Unwilling to argue with him in the car, she withdrew the key and handed it to him. Tension crackled in the air between them during the remainder of the drive to his hotel. Sitting in frozen silence beside him, Val seethed with impotent rage. Jonas was spoiling for a fight. She could feel the vibrations radiating from him.

Val had witnessed Jonas in a fight. She knew that, when geared for battle, Jonas was darned near invincible. Steeling herself for the coming confrontation, Val vowed that he would not win, at least not without knowing he'd been in the fight of his life.

Valerie had expected to be delivered to the stately old hotel where she and Jonas had spent their wedding night. Instead, the limo glided to a stop in front of a fairly new building. As she stepped from the car, Valerie glanced up at the clean, straight lines of the tower, rising majestically above the surrounding structures. In a way she was disappointed, as she had decided it would be fitting to conduct their argument in the same suite in which they had spent their aborted honeymoon.

Head high, her purpose firm, Val entered the hotel at Jonas's side. The suite that Jonas ushered her into was lavish, if not steeped in the elegance of the suite they had shared three years ago. It consisted of four rooms, a spacious sitting room, two large bedrooms and a connecting bathroom. The floor-to-ceiling draperies were drawn in the sitting room and the largest of the bedrooms, revealing floor-to-ceiling walls of glass. The night view of the lights of the city below and the bay beyond the windows was spectacular.

Dropping onto the settee the stole she'd worn against the evening damp and chill, Val walked to the wide expanse of window as if drawn by a magnet. "Beautiful," she whispered, transfixed by the panorama before her.

"Yes."

Val turned at the odd note in Jonas's voice. His expression puzzled her. What was he thinking? she wondered, experiencing an inexplicable thrill of anticipation.

"Beautiful" seemed barely adequate to describe her, Jonas thought, feeling his insides tighten. Val was stunning, breathtaking. In the setting of the night view behind her, Val stood out like a rare gem in a collection of unpolished stones.

She was wearing the off-the-shoulder, violet-hued chiffon gown she'd purchased for the occasion—the gown Jonas had decided had been designed to arouse male interest and admiration. The enticing way the chiffon draped her breasts, revealing just a hint of the gentle curves beneath, certainly succeeded in arousing him. Jonas felt his stomach clench at the thought of other men experiencing the same response to her fragile-looking beauty. Her only adornments were the filigree necklace and drop earrings he'd given her... and the rings encircling the third finger of her small left hand.

A flash of possessiveness streaked through Jonas as his gaze lingered on the gold band nestled beside the large solitaire diamond that appeared too heavy for her slender finger. Slowly he trailed his gaze up her body to confront her. Val was his, and he'd be damned if he'd let her get away from him. But this time he'd play it smart, Jonas decided. He'd blown his chance to make things right with her the night of the reception, while they were in the garden. He wouldn't make the same mistake again.

Val stood poised in front of the window wall, her facade of composure concealing a growing uneasiness. Jonas was so quiet, too quiet. A curl of excitement combined with her uneasiness to make an explosive mixture when he slowly examined her with his narrowed eyes. The silence lengthened, tearing at her nerves. Val was afraid that if Jonas didn't say something, and soon, she'd begin to unravel.

"It's time for us to talk."

Valerie started at the soft sound of his voice. Expecting him to attack with anger and impatience, she was confused by his reticence. Was she imagining things, or had she detected a hint of uncertainty underlying his quiet tone? Valerie hoped so, because she didn't like the idea of being the only uncertain person in the room. "I know," Val replied softly.

He didn't move for long seconds. Then, when he did, she jumped again. A wry smile twitched the corners of his lips. "Relax, sweetheart," he drawled. "I'm not going to pounce on you." Instead of walking toward her, Jonas strode to the small dining table that stood in one corner of the room. Picking up a large folder, he flipped it open. "I don't know about you, but I didn't have dinner and I'm hungry." He gave her an inquisitive look.

Not quite sure what to make of his mild manner, Val simply stared at him, trying to gauge his mood.

"Val, are you hungry?"

Now Val was really confused. Rather than impatient, Jonas actually seemed amused. Relieved, yet still suspicious, she answered, "Yes, a little. I didn't eat very much of my dinner."

Jonas grinned, and thoroughly rattled Val in the process. "The usual tasteless banquet chicken, huh?"

Stunned by his show of good humor, Val replied without thinking. "No, I think it was some sort of beef, but I really don't remember."

"Whatever." Jonas shrugged, and glanced down at the folder. "Let's see what room service has to offer."

"Jonas, it's nearly midnight," Val reminded him. "Isn't it too late for room service?"

"No," he murmured, intent on the menu. "This hotel offers twenty-four-hour room service. But it is too late for dinner. After eleven it's mostly snack foods, but they do have a selection of basket meals." Once again he glanced up to give her a questioning look.

Perfect, Val thought. A basket meal for a basket case. Distracted, she asked, "What's the basket meal?"

Jonas kept a straight face. "A basket meal, Valerie, is a meal contained in a basket."

"I know that!" Val flashed a quick, tremulous smile, and felt a spark of warmth flutter inside when Jonas inhaled sharply in response. "Ah..." She paused, trying to recall the subject. Food! Right. "What I'm asking is: what does the meal in the basket contain?"

Jonas laughed, spreading the warmth inside Val. "We have our choice of several," he answered, the low sexiness of his voice at variance with the mundane topic. "There are chicken fingers, burgers and their version of a Philly cheese steak," he recited, referring to the menu. "They all come with French fries and slaw on the side." Jonas raised his head and one eyebrow simultaneously. "You want to try the steak?"

"No thanks." Val gave him a knowing look and a brief shake of her head. "I've tried other places' versions of a Philly cheese steak. I'll wait till I get back to Philly and have the real thing." She thought it over for a moment, then decided, "I think I'll have a burger."

"Okay." Jonas reached for the phone.

"With cheese."

"Fine." He punched the room service number.

"And bacon."

He shot her a droll look. "Right."

"And lettuce and tomato and mayo."

Jonas lost control. Holding his palm over the receiver, he roared with laughter. "I thought you said you were only a little hungry?" he gasped as his laughter subsided.

With a nonchalance that belied the melting sensation his amusement induced within her, Val strolled to the settee. "That was fifteen minutes ago," she informed him with a regal air. "My appetite has sharpened since then."

"My appetite's pretty sharp, too," Jonas muttered before he responded to the prompting from room service.

His double-edged remark stole Val's breath and increased the melting sensation. Feeling suddenly lightheaded, boneless, she sank onto the settee. She didn't know what kind of game Jonas was playing, but then she didn't much care, either. Experiencing an odd, exciting sense of adventure, Val waited expectantly for whatever might develop.

After placing their order, Jonas circled the table to the long cabinet set against the wall. "The person in room service said it'll be about fifteen minutes. Would you like a drink while we wait?" He swung one cabinet door open to reveal two fully stocked shelves of bottles.

"Is there any white wine?" Val asked, smoothing the long chiffon skirt over her knees with trembling fingers.

Jonas gave her a dry look. "Of course. Had you seriously thought I'd forgotten that you never drink anything other than white wine?"

"No...." She hesitated, then confessed. "At least, I had hoped you hadn't forgotten." The issue was minor, yet Val was amazed how very important it was to her to hear that he had remembered.

"Hoped?" Jonas asked with a sigh. "Have I been so neglectful of you, Val, that you would even doubt?"

Tension slammed back into Val, robbing her of the heady sense of adventure and excitement. Disappointed, she lowered her eyes. "Jonas...I..."

"Never mind." Jonas spoke, not impatiently, but in a surprising, almost supplicating tone. "You don't have to say it, I know the answer." Then his voice changed, becoming brusque. "There's a bottle of champagne chilling in the fridge."

Val glanced up to see him swing open the door on the other side of the cabinet to reveal a small refrigerator, complete with ice trays and bottles of mixers, seltzers and mineral water. Reaching down, he removed a dark foil-capped bottle from the wine rack mounted on the door. After closing the door, he turned, smiling wryly as he held up the bottle for her inspection.

"Impressive," Val murmured at the sight of the imported label. "A meal of burgers served with champagne that costs one hundred and fifty dollars a bottle?"

Jonas shrugged. "Well, it's not the best," he said, turning to pick up two long-stemmed tulip glasses from the tray on top of the cabinet. "But it'll have to do." He removed the foil wrap and wire guard, then with a deft twist of his hand eased the cork from the bottle with a muted pop, without losing a drop of the bubbling contents.

He poured the golden liquid into the glasses and had started toward her when a light knock sounded on the door.

"Dinner?" Val guessed, holding out her hands in a silent offer to relieve him of the glasses.

Stepping to her, Jonas handed her the tulips, then turned toward the door. "Could be the driver with your cases."

It was. After the man had departed, Jonas carried the two suitcases into the bedroom...his bedroom. Setting the glasses on the low table in front of the settee, Val rose and trailed into the room after him. Jonas shot her a narrowed, challenging look as she entered.

"I, ah, think I'll change into something more casual," she said, hoping to keep the atmosphere between them defused by removing the gown that seemed to have an explosive effect on Jonas.

"No, don't," he said quickly, then continued with a suggestive smile. "At least, not until after dinner."

Val frowned in confusion. "But I thought you didn't like the gown, Jonas!"

Leaving the cases where he'd dropped them, Jonas came to her. Raising a hand, he caught a bit of the filmy material capping her shoulders and slid it between his fingers. "It's a beautiful gown, and even more beautiful on you, Val," he murmured. "What I didn't particularly like was having you wear it for anyone else but me."

Val went weak and swayed toward him. "Oh, Jonas."

Jonas brought up his other hand to grasp her shoulder as he slowly lowered his head to hers. Val could feel his moist breath against her mouth. The mood was shattered by another knock on the door and a muffled voice announcing: "Room service."

Jonas froze. He frowned. Then he swore.

Laughing softly, Val raised one hand and silenced him with a finger over his lips. "You get the door," she instructed, moving away from him. "I'll get the wine."

Glasses in her hands, Val stood patiently by as the waiter transferred the food and utensils from the serving cart to the table.

"I'll leave the cart by the door," he said, as Jonas ushered him from the room. "Just roll it into the hallway when you're finished."

"Fine," Jonas replied, bringing a wide smile to the man's face with a large tip. "And thank *you*." He shut the door firmly, cutting off the waiter's profuse thanks.

"You weren't very polite to the poor man," Val chastised Jonas laughingly, as he slid into the chair opposite her at the small table.

"But I was generous," Jonas retorted, raising his glass to her in a silent salute. "Now eat your dinner before it gets stone-cold."

Val accepted his salute by taking a sip of the wine, then murmured in obvious amusement, "Yes, sir, Mr. Thorne, sir."

Jonas grew still, the burger in his hands poised midway between the basket and his mouth.

"Jonas?" Val asked hesitantly, suddenly nervous again. "What is it? What's wrong?"

A faint smile, partly sad, partly reflective, played over his firm mouth. "Do you have any idea how long it's been since you've called me that in that irreverent, teasing tone?"

The nervous sensation changing to an altogether different feeling, Val took a deep breath and a hopeful guess. "Too long?"

Jonas sighed. "Much too long."

Val assumed guilt without question—like most wives? she wondered. "I'm sorry, Jonas."

"Yeah, so am I." He smiled derisively. "You're angry that I didn't tell you about the monthly payments to Lynn." It wasn't a question; he knew the answer.

"Yes," Val answered anyway. "Angry and hurt."

Jonas exhaled deeply. "I've thought it over, and finally realized that you have every right to be angry," he admitted, surprising Val. But before she could respond, he surprised her even more. "I'm sorry, too, Val," he continued. "I have no excuse. I honestly never even considered how it might concern you. It's meaningless." He offered her a wry smile. "I want you to believe that. I support Lynn for one reason and one reason only, and that is to keep her out of my hair."

Val was silent for a moment, during which she could see that Jonas looked strained and decidedly uncomfortable. Then, delighted to discover that she had the singular power to make the otherwise impervious Jonas Thorne squirm, she drew out the silence a little longer.

It was a battle of nerves; Jonas surrendered first, turning Val's surprise to utter amazement. "I wish you'd say something, anything," he muttered. "Even if it's only to give me hell."

"I believe I've tried that in the past," Val replied in a dry drawl. "It never did me much good."

Jonas actually winced. "I know I haven't been the easiest man to live with, but—"

Val's spontaneous burst of laughter cut him off. "The easiest?" she taunted. "Try the most difficult."

"Yeah." Jonas suddenly looked tired, and a little afraid. "You're bored, aren't you, Val?"

"Not with you!" Val cried at once, frightened by the defeated look on his strong face. "Never with you, Jonas."

"But with our life together?" he persisted. "With our life-style?"

Val broke the end off a golden-brown fry, then looked at it as though she'd never before seen its like. "Jonas, our life-style is . . ." Her voice trailed away, and she idly played with the bit of potato as she raked her mind for a way to express her feelings of inadequacy and frustration.

"Confining," Jonas finished for her.

Val lifted her head. She had entered the suite expecting an argument. When Jonas appeared intent on avoiding one, she had begun to hope they could discuss their problems without rancor or raised voices. But Val could not, would not back down from her position simply to fulfill that hope. "Yes, Jonas," she answered clearly. "I find our life-style confining."

Jonas had said he was starving, yet he had barely touched his food. As if suddenly becoming aware of the large burger he was holding, he raised it to his mouth. "Okay." After murmuring the single word, he nodded once and bit into the sandwich.

Okay? Val frowned. What did that mean? she asked herself. Okay . . . what? Okay, they'd change their life-style or . . . ? Val felt a flash of sheer panic. Surely he hadn't meant to imply that he'd be willing to end the marriage. Her thoughts darting here and there, Val absently picked up her burger and followed his example. He couldn't have meant that, she assured herself, chewing, swallowing, but not tasting anything except fear. Jonas was too possessive, too—

His terse voice sliced across her fractured thoughts. "Did you hear me, Val?"

"Y-yes." Val couldn't have controlled the tremor in her voice if her life had depended on it. "I heard. I— I'm just not sure I understand what you meant."

"I meant . . . Okay, I'll free you from the exclusive, confining role of being my housewife."

Panic ballooned inside Val, and she rushed to explain. "I don't mind the housework, Jonas, really I don't. It's just that it's not enough. I mean, I want to do more. I need to—"

Once again Jonas cut her off. "But if you're coming back to work, even if only on a part-time basis, I insist you hire someone to help with the housework."

"Coming back to work?" Val repeated, unable to believe she'd heard him correctly. "Jonas, I—"

Jonas interrupted her for the third time. "You don't think I'd allow you to work for a competitor, do you?" Picking up his glass, he tilted it at her. "I could use another assistant." Bringing the glass to his lips, he drank to her. "Do you want the job or not?"

"Want it?" Val stared at him in stunned amazement. "Jonas, you know I'd adore working with you again."

Jonas raised his eyebrows mockingly. "Really? I have it on good authority that I'm a bas—"

"Jonas," Val's warning voice overrode his.

He grinned. "A devil to work for," he finished, biting with relish into his sandwich.

This time Val deliberately followed his lead, and this time she tasted the burger. It was rather good. "What authority?" she asked after swallowing the morsel.

"The best," Jonas replied blandly, popping a fry into his mouth. "You."

"Did I say that?" Val asked in feigned innocence, beginning to enjoy herself. In fact, she realized, she was beginning to feel wonderful.

"Mmm." Jonas nodded, his eyes teasing her over the burger he'd just bitten into.

"Fancy that."

"I fancy you."

Val melted. "Oh, Jonas, I fancy you, too. You'll never know how unhappy and depressed I've been from all the discord and bitterness between us."

His smile was wry. "I have a pretty good idea." He reached a hand across the table, palm up. An audible sigh of relief whispered through his lips when she slid her hand into his. "Oh, God, I've missed you, Val."

"I missed you, too." Val could barely speak around the emotion gripping her throat.

"The house was empty." Jonas shuddered. "I was empty."

"I know." Val blinked.

"Can you forgive me for being such an arrogant, unsympathetic ass the past three years?"

"Yes." Val smiled mistily. "If you can forgive me for driving you crazy with all my courses and projects."

Jonas grimaced. "You did have me going around in circles."

"I'm sorry."

Jonas gave a quick bark of laughter. "No, you're not."

Val's grin was shaky, but there. "I did manage to get your attention."

"You did at that." His hand tightened convulsively around hers. "I love you, Val."

"I love you, Jonas."

"Finish your dinner, Val." Jonas's voice grew low, sensuous, enticing. "You're going to need your strength for the dessert I have in mind."

"Yes, sir, Mr. Thorne," Val whispered. "Anything you say, anything you want, sir."

His smile was beautiful.

Chapter Seven

Inspired by Jonas's smile, Val managed to finish most of her food, and all of the wine in the glass he kept refilling until the bottle was empty.

But it wasn't the wine that went to Val's senses, it was the man seated opposite her, devouring her with his eyes every bit as thoroughly as he devoured every bite of his burger, French fries and slaw.

Jonas had opened his bow tie and the two top buttons of his shirt midway through the meal. Although Val had lived with him for three years, had seen him naked nearly every night of those years, for some inexplicable reason she found the sight of those two strips of black silk lying against the pristine white of his dress shirt as sexy as the devil he had earlier said he was reputed to be.

If Jonas was a devil in the office, Val mused, watching him polish off her fries as well as his own, he was an even more effective devil in bed. A thrill glided from her nape to the base of her spine. And it had all begun for them here in San Francisco, three years ago. Then she had shivered for a different reason, Val reflected.

Though she had worked in the office with him as his secretary, Val hadn't known Jonas very well. And what she did know of him—his arrogance, his impatience—hadn't endeared him to her. Jonas had bargained with her over their marriage, but when it came to the crunch on their wedding night, Val had been more than nervous. She'd been scared witless.

A smile lurked at the corners of Val's mouth as she remembered the delaying tactics she had tried to employ to escape the inevitable . . . all to no avail. Jonas had humored her for a time, then he had reached his limit. He had taken a wife, and had every intention of taking her as his wife.

What had she expected? Val's smile was shaded with self-mockery. She knew full well, had known that night, what she'd expected. She had both feared and expected that he would take her arrogantly, impatiently.

Foolish woman, Val silently chided her younger self. In an elegant hotel suite, less than a mile away from where she now sat sipping her wine and drinking in the exciting sight of her husband, that younger Val had stood shivering in fear of the man she now loved more than her own life.

Oh, Jonas had taken her as his wife, Val reminisced. But he had taken her gently, sensuously, caressing her with exquisite torture until she had grown wild with the hungry need to be one with him.

Even after three years and all the problems they'd encountered in simply living together, the memory of that night retained the power to turn Valerie's insides to the consistency of melting cream.

Observing him over the rim of her glass with betraying, smoldering eyes, Val acknowledged that she still was wild with a hungry need to be one with him.

"What's going on inside that beautiful head of yours, I wonder?" Jonas murmured, scattering her thoughts, intensifying the thrill in her body. "You're wearing the most intriguing, sexy little smile on your inviting mouth."

"Is my mouth inviting, Jonas?"

His lips curved in appreciative amusement. "Don't change the subject. What were you thinking about?"

Val swept her eyelashes downward, demurely, enticingly. "I was remembering our wedding night." The thrill spread up to the back of her head, making her scalp tingle, and she heard him catch his breath.

"It was a fantastic night."

"You said we'd come back to San Francisco someday for a repeat performance," she reminded him.

Jonas's voice was low, sensuous. "We're here now."

"Yes."

A teasing note enhanced his tone. "Is it time for dessert, Val?"

Val raised her eyes to his. "Yes."

"Since we're in the state of make-believe, should I sweep you up into my arms in true Hollywood fashion and carry you into our bedroom?"

"Good Lord, no!" Val exclaimed with a laugh. "I think you should help me clear the table and roll the room service cart into the corridor. Then we'll walk into the bedroom together, in true husband and wife fashion."

Jonas shoved back his chair. "Then let's get to it." He grinned suggestively. "So we can get to it."

With the reward of pleasure as incentive, Val and Jonas made quick work of clearing away the dishes. Then, while he rolled the cart into the hallway, Val drifted into the bedroom, drawn once more by the expanse of windows overlooking the sleeping city. It was late, very late, and considering how tired she'd been earlier, Val should have felt exhausted. She didn't. Quite the contrary, she felt wide-awake and elated.

Spread out before her, the gold-toned city lights appeared muted and dimmed by the billowing shroud of fog rolling in from the bay. Rather than feeling chilled by the sight of the creeping mist, Val felt removed from the damp and the cold, warm and protected, not by the heated suite, but by Jonas's indomitable presence.

"I thought the plan was for us to walk into the bedroom together." The direct cause of Val's feeling of comfort spoke from the bedroom doorway.

Her expression dreamy, her smile alluring, Val slowly turned to look at him. "I stood before a window overlooking San Francisco on a night three years ago," she murmured. "Remember, Jonas?"

"Yes." Though Jonas didn't move, his soft voice crept across the room to envelop Val in warm sensuality, clouding her mind as completely as the fog clouded the city. "You were wearing a chiffon gown then, too. You stole my breath and my heart, and infuriated me by trying to superimpose another man's form over mine." His voice grew softer with compassion. "Do you remember, Valerie?"

"Yes." Val's smile was tinged with remembered sadness and gratitude. "I told you I had loved him . . . and I begged you to understand. You did."

"I tried. It wasn't easy." Jonas shrugged and moved into the room. "I wanted you so much," he whispered as he came to her. "And I wanted you to want me, too."

"It didn't take you long to achieve that goal," Val confessed with a shiver of remembrance.

Jonas trailed his fingers over her cheek. "And then having you want me wasn't enough. I wanted you to love me."

"I do." With a sense of awe, Val felt the tremor that rippled through his body to his fingertips.

"And then," Jonas went on in a voice rough with self-condemnation, "like a fool, I ran the risk of losing what I value most—you and your love for me."

"No, Jonas," Val denied with soft vehemence. "Never, *never* that."

"Oh, God, Val," Jonas groaned, pulling her into his arms. "Hold me. Don't ever let me go."

Sliding her arms around his neck, Val clung to him fiercely as he bent over her. "I won't, darling," she promised, lifting her face to his.

Jonas shuddered at the sound of the endearment, then crushed her mouth with his. His lips were hard. His kiss tasted of desperation. Clinging to him, Val answered to his need.

Without haste, between lingering kisses and inflaming caresses, they undressed each other, pausing to kiss, stroke, adore each newly exposed area of heated flesh.

And then, when his elegant tuxedo lay where Jonas had tossed it, on the floor atop the delicate violet chiffon of Val's gown, and they were both trembling with desire, Jonas did sweep Val into his arms, Thorne fashion, and carried her to the bed. He stared down at her for several seconds after settling her on the mattress, then whispering of his love for her, his need of her, Jonas covered his wife's shivering form with the blanketing warmth of his body.

Murmuring his name, Val welcomed Jonas into the haven of her silken embrace and cradling thighs. His possession was swift and hard and complete. Val wouldn't have had it any other way. Enticing him with biting kisses, raking fingernails and mewing moans deep in her throat, she arched into his thrusting body, not merely accepting but demanding the shattering joy of release and completion.

"Was I too rough, my love?" Jonas asked, stroking one broad palm over the satiny skin of her hip.

Val smiled and moved her body luxuriously against the length of his. "You were more than rough. You were magnificent," she responded, almost purring, undulating her hips in time with the motions of his caressing hand.

His low laughter had the exciting dark sound of satisfaction and pleasure. "And you were the perfect match for me," he murmured, sparking a delicious new shiver inside her. "I'm positive I'll carry your branding claw marks to my grave."

The shiver turned to ice and Val jolted back to stare at him with concern-widened eyes. "Did I hurt you?"

"Hurt?" His laughter whispered into a sigh. "Oh, sweetheart, the only way you could ever hurt me is by holding back, denying me the passion commanding your response."

Her fear eased, Val shimmied her body along the angular length of his, her parted lips reaching for his mouth. "Was I good for you, Jonas?" she whispered, dropping tiny kisses over his collarbone.

"No," he growled, skimming his hands from her hips to her hair. "You were deliciously bad."

Her soft laughter ended on a gasp as he tangled his fingers in her hair and tugged back her head, exposing her throat to his searching mouth.

"You like that?" Jonas asked, probing the hollow at the base of her throat with the tip of his tongue.

"Yesss." The response hissed through her lips on a sigh.

Arching her back, he trailed his tongue to the valley between her breasts. "And that?"

"Yes." This time her response was short, a mere puff of breath.

Continuing his exploration, Jonas slid his tongue to the crest of one arching breast. "I guess I don't have to ask if you like that," he said with a chuckle, feeling the shudder that quaked through her.

"Jonas...Jonas..." Val chanted, gripping his shoulders convulsively. "Please..."

"No, not yet," he murmured. Releasing her hair, he eased her onto her back. "Lie still, darling. Don't move. Let me show you how much I love you." Holding her delicate wrists in one large hand, he drew out her arms straight over her head.

"Jonas?" Val flexed her fingers, revealing her need, her desire to touch him.

"Relax, love." His crooning voice slowed the urgency racing through her body. "This is for you."

Jonas began by touching his lips to the pulse that was hammering in her wrist. Then, murmuring new endearments, he strung soft kisses down her arm. Within seconds, Val drifted into a state of liquid warmth. Her thundering heartbeat slowly decreased its rate, her breathing grew regular, her eyes closed, the fire inside her body burned low. Her mind floated, dancing to the rhythms of his downy kisses and the feather-light caresses of his hands.

It was incredible. Val ached, but the ache was sweet. She hungered, but the hunger was teasing. She yearned, but the yearning held promise. Val had never before experienced anything quite like this sedating seduction. Jonas didn't make love to her, he worshiped her. He didn't caress her, he adored her. With his mouth, his hands and his low, intense murmurs, Jonas cherished Val's body, mind and soul.

When he came to her, into her, Val enfolded Jonas within the living beauty of her love for him.

* * *

When Val awoke, the sun was shining. Her world was beautiful, because Jonas was there, stroking her, soothing her, loving her. His power over her was complete; she was his to command. In the light of that acknowledgement, his very first words to her were enslaving.

"Good morning. I adore you."

Tears brightened her eyes and clung to her inky lashes. "Oh, Jonas, I love you so very much." She gazed at him, her love shining from her eyes as brightly as the sunlight sparkling outside. "And I'm so sorry."

"Sorry?" Jonas narrowed his eyes. "Sorry for what?"

"I accused you of being possessive," she answered. "And now I'm sorry for not realizing that in your own way you were caring for me."

His smile was a little tender, a little self-derisive. "I didn't realize it, either."

"That you were caring for me?"

"No. That in your own way *you* were caring for me." He shook his head. "I didn't really appreciate the care you took, keeping me well fed and comfortable, armored to face each and every day, good, bad or indifferent." He gave her a chiding smile. "Now that I do realize it, I'm almost sorry I offered you the job of part-time assistant."

"But that's the beauty of it, my love!" Val exclaimed. "Don't you see that now I can care for you in the office, as well as at home?"

Jonas laughed and hugged her to him. "At the risk of repeating myself, I adore you, Valerie Thorne."

Val planted a smacking kiss somewhere in the vicinity of his laughing mouth. "And I love you, Jonas Thorne, sir."

"That's all I want," he said, lifting a hand to gently stroke away a teardrop lingering on her lashes. "Having your love is all I need to survive."

"And that's all?" she asked in teasing awe.

"Well," Jonas drawled. "Maybe that...and some breakfast." Grinning wickedly, he hauled her on top of him. "But let's have the loving first, then the breakfast."

Valerie and Jonas spent one laughter-filled, love-drenched week in San Francisco, enjoying the honeymoon they had never had, the honeymoon they would have been too uncertain of each other to enjoy if they had had it three years ago.

Valerie gained four pounds. Jonas lost the lines of strain around his mouth. She looked sleek and content. He appeared vital and energized. They turned heads wherever they went. They went just about everywhere.

Jonas took her dancing. Val took him shopping along the wharf. He escorted her through Chinatown. She guided him through art galleries. They rented a car and drove down the coast, through Big Sur and into Los Angeles. There they boarded a flight back to San Francisco.

And for the first time in three years of marriage, they took the time to talk...and talk...and talk.

"She's like a child, you know," Jonas said at one point, when Lynn's name was mentioned. "A selfish, greedy child. In intellect, if not in years, she is younger than Mary Beth. But Lynn is her mother, and for Mary Beth I'll tolerate her."

"Of course," Val replied, at last fully understanding his position. "And so will I."

"Oh, Jonas, the exhibitions were dreadful," Val confessed at another point, when he asked about the rally. "I knew I had wasted my time after five minutes of the first event."

"So why didn't you come home?" Jonas growled.

"I was being independent," Val admitted. "Besides, I didn't want to face an 'I told you so' look from you."

Jonas laughed. "You should've braved my expression. You could have saved the office from the beast."

"Were you being a brute, love?" Val inquired, delighted by the idea of him being as miserable without her as she had been without him.

"No, I was being a regular bas—"

"Jonas."

"Basket case," he finished with an unrepentant grin at the warning in her tone.

"Where am I going to work?" Val asked, cuddling as close as she could get to him in the seat of the plane as the Lear jet streaked eastward.

Without ceremony, Jonas hauled her from her seat and settled her on his lap. "I was thinking about the room separating my office from Charlie's."

"The one used for storage?"

"Mmm." Jonas nodded. "Would that be big enough?"

Thrilled at the prospect of being situated just a few steps down the hall from him, Val said eagerly, "That'll be fine. When can I start?"

"It'll have to be cleared out and decorated," Jonas said, weighing the possibilities. "How about, say, a month?"

Fully aware of how quickly Jonas could get a job accomplished if he was determined to have it done, Val gave him an arched look. "How about one week?"

"Two." Jonas grinned, obviously enjoying the new sensation of bargaining with her.

"Ten days," Val said, returning his grin, telling him she was enjoying herself as much as he was.

"You win." Then, just as her grin slipped into laughter, he added, "This time."

It was Friday. It was late. It was quiet. The weather was warm and fine. Eager to commence their summer weekend, the employees of J.T. Electronics had left the building over an hour before. The place was deserted except for the security personnel...and the boss.

A smile of satisfaction easing the firm line of his mouth, Jonas stood in the doorway of the newly refurbished office. Thanks to the generous bonus he had offered the work crew he'd hired to renovate the storage room, the office was finished, five days ahead of schedule.

Jonas felt a surge of anticipation as he slowly ran his gaze over the interior of the room.

Taking precious time from his schedule, Jonas had personally chosen the decor. Now he couldn't wait to tell Val about *her* office.

Why should he wait? Jonas asked himself. Both his smile and feeling of anticipation growing, he turned away and strode the few steps to his own office suite. Using his private line he punched out his home number and drummed his long fingers impatiently on the desk top while the connection was made. The phone at home rang and rang. On the fourth ring, Jonas curled his fingers into his palm in frustration.

Damn it! Where was she? Even as he fired the question at himself there came a click. At the breathless sound of Val's voice, he redirected the question at her.

"Where the hell were you?"

"Right here," Val replied, unruffled by his impatient tone. "Where the hell are you?"

Jonas suppressed an urge to laugh. His wife was picking up his bad habits...and his language. "I'm still in the office," he said in a much milder tone.

"Why?"

Jonas shot a glance at his watch, the new one Val had given him for his birthday. It had been a belated gift, arriving the day after they'd returned from the West Coast. It was fashioned in mat gold, elegant in its simplicity. In that flashing instant, Jonas could see with his mind's eye the message Val had had inscribed on the back. There were two dates, those of their wedding and of that memorable first night they'd spent together in San Francisco. Jonas treasured the gift, as he treasured its giver.

It wasn't past his usual time for leaving the office. He frowned and replied, "Why what?"

"Why aren't you here with me?" Val asked softly. "When the phone rang, I was in the shower—" her voice dropped even lower "—and missing you."

The image that sprang into Jonas's mind displaced every other thought. He forgot his intention of asking her to come to the complex to see her new office. He forgot the report he had planned to skim over before calling it a day. All he could think about was Val with her hair pinned up, water cascading over her slender form.

"I'll be home in fifteen minutes," he promised, the huskiness in his voice betraying the sudden tightness in his body. "Keep the water running."

"It'll get cold."

"I won't."

"Drive carefully, darling," Val cautioned. "I want you in one piece."

Jonas groaned. "No comment."

Jonas walked away from his desk without a second thought or backward glance. He drove his car into the driveway exactly fourteen minutes after hanging up the phone.

Val was waiting. She swung the door open as he loped along the flagstone walk to the front of the house. Her hair was not, as he'd imagined, pinned up. It tumbled in a mass of loose curls on her shoulders. From neck to ankles she was covered in a belted robe, the picture of modesty. But the toes peeping out from beneath the hem of her robe were bare. Jonas fervently hoped the rest of her body was the same.

Stepping over the threshold, he pulled her to him with one arm and shut the door with the other. When her soft curves conformed pliantly to the hard angles of his body, Jonas knew he was home. He didn't bother with a verbal greeting. Lowering his head, he said hello by crushing her raised mouth with his own.

"What are you wearing under your robe?" he murmured, ending the kiss, but maintaining contact by brushing his mouth over her lips.

"Expectations," Val breathed, bringing her hands up to frame his face.

Jonas's blood raced, he was immediately hot and tight and more than ready to fulfill her slightest whim. "And what are they?" he asked, teasing her by holding his mouth a sigh away from hers.

"I'll tell you after dinner," Val promised, teasing him in return.

"The hell with dinner." Sweeping her into his arms, Jonas mounted the stairs. "I'll have 'dessert' first."

Jonas groaned a sigh as he slid into her satin warmth. For a moment he didn't move, savoring the sensations streaking through his body. Making love with Val had always been better than good. Since San Francisco, it was better than fantastic.

"Jonas."

He shivered, both at the enticing sound of her voice and the inflaming caress of her silken thighs gliding slowly around his hips. Obeying her plea, Jonas began to move, stoking her passion and his own as he drove deeper and yet deeper into the heart of her desire.

Jonas was trembling outside, quaking inside from the intensity of need consuming his body. His teeth were clenched and the tendons in his neck were rigid from the strain he was exerting on his control. Conflicting desires warred inside him. While part of him screamed to let go, to surrender to the blazing joy of release, another part of him fought to hang on, drawing out the sweetness of pleasure to the point of pain.

Strong tremors rippled through his muscles wherever Val's restless hands paused to stroke and caress. His breathing grew ragged; his skin grew moist. Still he held on to his control, wringing delicious agony from the pleasure.

When, at Val's moaning plea, Jonas relinquished control, he cried out her name as he was flung into the fiery center of his exploding senses.

"Are you ready for dinner now?" Val murmured teasingly a while later, as she smoothed back his hair from his damp brow.

"Do I have to get up?" he muttered, groaning as he heaved himself onto the mattress beside her. At that moment, Jonas felt positive he'd never move again.

"No, of course not." Val's tone of unconcern had him prying one eyelid open. "I'll serve you dinner in bed," she said agreeably, sliding off the side of the bed. "But first I'll take a shower." She sighed and glanced over her shoulder at him as she went toward the bathroom. "All by myself."

Jonas was off the bed and after her as if he'd been shot from a cannon. "Vixen," he growled when she evaded his hands. But his growl turned to a purr beneath the soothing shower spray and the gentle ministrations of his laughing wife.

"Did we ruin dinner by lingering over dessert?" Jonas asked, tucking a short-sleeved sport shirt into his pants.

"No." Val's voice was muffled by the silky knit top she was pulling over her head. "Since it's Friday," she continued, smoothing the blouse over her skirt, "I was hoping to beguile you into taking me out for dinner." Tossing him a coaxing smile, she slipped onto the velvet padded stool in front of her vanity table.

Jonas fastened his watchband before crossing to her. "Lady," he said to her reflection in the lighted mirror, "You are one expert beguiler." He didn't mention that her suggestion fitted in neatly with his plans for the evening. "Where would you like to go to eat . . . and do I have to change again?"

Val paused, one hand raised, her fingers gripping a mascara wand, and ran a comprehensive look over his image in the glass. "No." She shook her head and smiled. "You look devastating in casual clothes."

"Devastating?" Jonas laughed. "After that workout a few minutes ago," he drawled, "don't you mean devastated?"

Finished applying her makeup, Val set down the wand and picked up a hair brush. "It was rather invigorating, wasn't it?" She stroked the brush through the strands Jonas had tangled with his fingers. "I'm starving."

Jonas grinned and plucked the brush from her hand. "Let me," he murmured, gently drawing the brush through the long strands, still damp and gleaming from the shower.

"Mmm." Val sighed with pleasure. "That feels lovely. You're spoiling me, Jonas."

"I'm working at it, darling," he murmured, sliding her hair to one side to expose her nape to his mouth.

"Heavenly," Val breathed, shivering in response.

"Dinner," Jonas said decisively, backing away from her while he still could.

They dined on broiled seafood and icy mugs of beer in a local tavern with a reputation for excellent meals and a friendly atmosphere. While they ate, Jonas asked Val about her day and told her some of the details of his own, which in itself said reams about the increasing depth of their relationship. Never before had he discussed anything other than the most trivial things about his business.

"I'm going to stop by the office before we go home," he said casually over coffee. "I want to pick up a report to read—" he grinned "—sometime over the weekend."

Val looked stunned. "You're not going into the office this weekend?"

Jonas smiled with wry humor. He understood her amazement; he had always gone into the office on the weekend, if only on Saturday, both before and since their marriage. But since returning from San Francisco the previous Sunday, he had reorganized his thinking. Jonas was still dedicated—no, addicted—to his work. He had simply decided that from now on, if there was work to be done over the weekend, as he knew there invariably would be, he'd do it at home at the convenience of his wife. He told her so, enjoying the changing expressions on her face, which ranged from amazement to sheer delight.

Val bombarded Jonas with questions during the short drive to the office building. Since she barely paused for breath, never mind waiting for an answer from him, he kept his responses to murmurs and grunts laced with amusement.

"Does this mean I can actually look forward to tripping over you in the house on weekends?"

"Mmm."

"Jonas! Do you think we might steal a whole weekend away every so often?"

"Sure."

In love with her, enthralled with her, Jonas smiled and listened as Val went on and on with questions in the same vein, until they arrived at their destination.

"Want to come along and see how the work's progressing on your office?" he asked casually as he brought the car to a stop.

"Of course!" Val exclaimed, jumping out of the vehicle. "I can't wait for it to be finished," she went on as the elevator swept them to the sixth floor.

Jonas smiled and ushered her along the carpeted corridor to the closed door a few steps down the hall from his suite. "Let me go first," he said, stepping in front of her to block her view. "There might be ladders left standing or something." He opened the door, reached inside to flick the light switch, then stepped aside to watch her reaction. It was immediate, vocal and extremely satisfying.

"Oh, Jonas, it's finished." Val's cry came out in a choked whisper. "And it's beautiful! How did you manage it? I mean, you've only had five days and . . . oh, Jonas, thank you!" Spinning around, she flung herself into his arms. For Jonas, that was even more satisfying.

Later that night, satisfied now in body as well as in spirit, Jonas lay awake, cradling his sleeping wife in his arms. He was relaxed and thoughtful. Val had been more thrilled with her office than she'd been with any of the luxuries he'd given her. And all because he had finally agreed to share a portion of his working life with her.

Incredible. Val loved him, truly, honestly, unconditionally loved him. Jonas closed his eyes and thanked God for the inner wisdom that had sent him to California. He had thought he had been happy before, but only now did he realize the magnitude of true happiness.

Val loved him.

The work was demanding. The boss was at times a tyrant. Val loved it . . . and him. It was the end of her second week in her new office. After the expected interval of confusion, Val was settling in, getting back into the swing of the electronics business.

Although her job description was different than when she'd manned the desk as Jonas's secretary, and the work more involved, she was beginning to get a handle on it.

Val had received invaluable help from Charlie, Janet and Jean-Paul, but the biggest and best assistance had come from her employer and husband.

Val was so happy that sometimes, if she allowed herself to think about it, it scared her. So she seldom allowed herself to think about it. She simply felt and rejoiced in the feeling.

Living with Jonas, sleeping with Jonas, had been wonderful, even when it wasn't so great. But living, sleeping and working with Jonas was as close to perfection as Val could ever hope to get, and so far it had all been great. A day didn't pass that Val didn't thank God for the defiant determination that had sent her to San Francisco.

Val was holding a prayer close to her heart. She had missed her normal cycle the week before. Hope bubbled like champagne inside her—hope that, as she had on their wedding night, she had conceived Jonas's child on the night of their reconciliation in San Francisco.

But Val was being cautious, rational. Her life had changed dramatically over the previous three weeks, in numerous ways. Any one of those changes could have tipped the balance of her inner clock. Val hadn't said a word to Jonas. She felt it would be cruel to build his hopes, only to dash them again if she was wrong. She decided to wait and pray.

It was Friday again—the end of Val's third week on the job. She was tired, but that wasn't unusual. Lately Val was always tired. She didn't mind. She knew excessive weariness was one of the first symptoms of pregnancy. She wanted to sleep a lot, which was the reason she had switched from working mornings to coming into the office after lunch.

The weekend beckoned with the alluring promise of rest. Pushing aside the contract she'd been studying, Val stretched her cramped back muscles and glanced at her watch. It was six-twenty. Collecting her purse and the attaché case Jonas had given her at breakfast on the morning of her first day of work, Val slid her chair away from her desk.

Her step firm, her small jaw set with purpose, Val walked through the empty outer office and into the private domain of the boss. Jonas was bent over the design table near the large window, poring over computer spread sheets.

"Okay, warden, how much?"

Jonas looked up, a distracted frown tugging together his ash-blond brows. "Warden? How much? Val, what in the world are you talking about?"

Val kept a straight, stern face. "The bond," she explained, tapping her foot impatiently. "How much will it cost me to spring my husband from this electronic prison?"

Jonas's brow cleared. Obviously fighting a smile, he worked his chiseled features into stern lines that were much more intimidating than hers. "You do realize, madam, that I can only issue a weekend pass for your husband?" he intoned severely. "You will have to return him to this cell by eight o'clock on Monday morning."

Val fought a bubble of delighted laughter but lost the battle. A Jonas who was not only willing to be interrupted from his work, but ready to contribute to as well as participate in her silly games, was too new an experience for her. Laughing, she dropped her purse and case and ran across the room into his open arms.

"What time is it?" Jonas asked, rubbing his cheek against her silky hair.

Raising her left arm, Val glanced at her wristwatch. "Six thirty-two exactly."

"That's right!" Jonas said in exaggerated exclamation. "And for giving the correct answer, you, Mrs. Valerie Thorne, of Philadelphia, Pennsylvania, have won the grand prize!"

"Which is?" Val laughed as she posed the question.

"A kiss from the boss." Dipping his head, Jonas covered her open mouth with his.

As prizes went, Val thought fuzzily, his kiss *was* pretty grand. The sensuous play of his tongue, however, was evocative of a different, grander prize.

"Mmm," Val murmured when he raised his head a fraction, ending the kiss but maintaining contact by nibbling on her lower lip. "That tasted like more."

Jonas lifted his head to look at her. "More leads to more," he said in teasing warning.

"That's okay." Val smiled and pressed herself to his tautening body. "It's after business hours."

"Watch it, sweetheart," he growled. "Or you might suddenly find yourself on your back on that couch over there. It's happened before.... If you remember?"

Remember! How could she forget? Val thought, shivering with the memory. It had happened in the early evening of the day she'd returned from Australia. Because the secretary who had replaced Val had quit without notice, a competent replacement hadn't been found. Since Val had not returned by the promised date, Jonas had been in a foul mood.

Acting on Janet's advice, Valerie had offered her assistance. She and Jonas had worked throughout the day in an atmosphere of tense truce. Somewhere around seven Val had had enough. She was tired and hungry. Marching into his office, she had demanded to know if he was planning to buy her dinner. Jonas had replied that he would, if that was what she wanted. Suddenly cautiously excited, Val had responded by asking him if he was inferring that he would be willing to give her anything she wanted. Jonas had softly countered by saying he would...if she would give him the single thing *he* wanted. When Val asked him what it was, Jonas had indicated the long white couch that still stood against the wall in his office.

"I want you, now, on that couch."

His words seemed to echo in Valerie's mind as if Jonas had just said them to her. His low laughter interrupted her reverie, and Val realized with a jolt that he had repeated aloud the demand he'd made three years before.

The effect of Val's scandalized expression was ruined by the twitch of amusement at the corners of her mouth. "Jonas, really," she scolded. "Aren't you ashamed?"

"No more than I was the other time." Jonas grinned. "But as a matter of fact, I'm even hotter and more ready to..."

"Jonas!" Val laughed as she spoke his name and slipped away from him. She held up a hand when he started after her. "Have you forgotten that we are due at your daughter's at eight?"

His only response was to scowl and utter a muttered curse.

"Tsk, tsk." Val clicked her tongue. "If I recall correctly, you were the one who agreed to join Mary Beth and Jean-Paul this evening for a friendly game of penny ante poker."

Jonas's scowl gave way to a wicked smile. "I'd much sooner stay home and play strip poker with you."

"So would I," Val admitted, a responsive shiver going through her. He took a step toward her, she took a step back. "But we can't. Mary Beth, Jean-Paul and Marge are expecting us."

Jonas exhaled a deep, exaggerated sigh and slanted a mournful glance at the white couch. Laughing at him, Val took his hand to lead him from the office.

"Come on, Jonas, I'll let you buy me dinner."

Jonas stopped in his tracks. His eyes glittered with devilry as he echoed the words she'd said to him that same evening over three years ago. "It'll cost you."

Val proved how good her own memory was by repeating the response he'd given to her. "Name your price."

Jonas managed to keep a straight face. "I want your promise that no matter how late it is when we get home tonight, you and I will have a little game of strip poker." He destroyed the effect of his somber look by wiggling his eyebrows at her.

Laughing, Val quoted his final words of long ago, "You've got it."

Val and Jonas didn't bother going home. They stopped for dinner at an out-of-the-way restaurant located less than a mile from their former home. The establishment had been in existence for over a hundred years. The decor was early American, warm and homey. Val couldn't help but recall that, close though they had lived to the place, the only time they had ever been there had been for a birthday dinner for Marge.

They dined on game pie prepared from an original recipe, a full-bodied burgundy and apple cobbler. And while they fed the hunger of their bodies, they replenished the deeper need of the soul with soft, intimate conversation.

Finally replete, they reluctantly left the restaurant, Val's hand securely clasped inside Jonas's, and went on to spend a laughter-filled evening with Mary Beth, Jean-Paul and Marge.

It was late before the penny ante game broke up. Pleased with herself for having won two dollars and fourteen cents, Val cheerfully pitched in with the cleaning up. The look of smoldering promise in the eyes Jonas swept over her was all the incentive Val needed to work swiftly.

Marge went into the kitchen to stack the glasses and snack food bowls in the dishwasher, while Val and Mary Beth replaced the lacy cloth and flower centerpiece on the dining-room table, at which the games had been played.

The phone rang, and Mary Beth and Jean-Paul exchanged frowning expressions.

"Now, who in the world...?" Mary Beth began, turning away to answer the call on the phone in the living room, but at that moment it stopped ringing.

"I suppose Marge answered it," Jean-Paul observed with a shrug. "We'll soon know...."

Suddenly they heard a scream from the kitchen.

"Oh, God! Jonas!" Marge called in a cry of agony. "Pick up the extension! Lynn was injured in an automobile accident! She's in critical condition in a hospital in Paris!"

Chapter Eight

Jonas was going to Paris. They were all going to Paris—Marge, Mary Beth and Jean-Paul. Only Val was staying at home.

"This shouldn't take very long." Jonas tossed a couple of shirts onto the bed near the open suitcase. "I figure two, three days at the most."

It was late, or early, depending on how one viewed it. At 4:00 a.m. on a Saturday morning, with weariness dragging down her spirit, Val didn't view it at all.... She endured it.

"Okay." The exhaustion in her voice was at odds with the competence of her movements as she neatly folded each shirt before placing it in the case.

"You're not angry?" Jonas came to a stop beside her, three neckties dangling from his fingers. Val could actually feel the tension in him.

"Angry?" Val looked up to offer him a faint smile. "No, Jonas, I'm not angry."

"But you do understand why I feel I must go?"

Val caught her lower lip between her teeth. She thought she understood. She was trying to understand. But she was so tired. A soft sigh escaped her guard. "I think so." She blinked against the hot sting of tears in her eyes. Tears of weariness, she told herself. That was all they were. "I want to understand, Jonas. It's just that—" The tears crested the barrier of her eyelids. "Why you?" she cried. "Why is it always you?" She lifted her hands, then let them fall. "I didn't miss the fact that Marge called out for you . . . not Mary Beth or Jean-Paul, but you. Whenever there's a crisis or even a minor problem, everyone turns to you to solve whatever it is."

"I have to go, Val."

"But why in this instance? Lynn is not your responsibility, Jonas," she argued. "Why must you go? Can't Jean-Paul handle whatever must be handled, if . . . ?" Val couldn't force herself to say *if Lynn dies*.

Jonas had no problem saying it. "You mean if Lynn doesn't make it?"

Val nodded in response.

Jonas's nod reflected hers. "In that event, Jean-Paul could handle it. But that possibility isn't the only consideration. Whether Lynn lives or dies, there will be arrangements to make and bills to pay." He grimaced. "More than likely, very large bills to pay."

"But Jean-Paul could—"

"Val," Jonas interrupted her. "I must go myself. My only child is pregnant. Her mother may be dying. Mary Beth is going to need the support of both her husband and me. Besides—" his tone took on an edge of determination "—this is a family matter. My family. And you're wrong. It is *my* responsibility, not Jean-Paul's. I'll take care of it myself."

Of course. There it was, the secret vulnerability that Jonas took great pains to conceal. Val had had a hint of the presence of that sensitive area while they were in San Francisco, when he had told her that he continued to tolerate Lynn because she was Mary Beth's mother. Val now understood that his feelings ran much deeper than that.

Jonas was a bastard. He had never known either one of his parents, since his mother had died at his birth and his father's identity was a mystery. As a ward of the court, Jonas had been placed in a succession of foster homes, most of them bad. Until he met and married Lynn, and had been accepted wholeheartedly by her parents, Marge and Stosh Kowalski, Jonas had never had a family. Subsequently, even though his marriage began to disintegrate almost at once, the birth of his child had emphasized Jonas's need to maintain *his* family.

Staring at him with compassion, Val now acknowledged that she should have recognized or at least suspected the depth of that need in Jonas before they were married, when he'd told her that his former mother-in-law had lived with him since Mary Beth was an infant.

Jonas would take care of his own, his family, Val realized. With an unconscious gesture she slid one hand over her abdomen. Being the man he was, Jonas would naturally extend that care to all of them, even Lynn, a family member whom he merely tolerated.

The absentminded, protective movement of her splayed hand did not go unnoticed.

"Val, are you all right?" Jonas asked with quick concern, bringing up his hands to grasp her shoulders.

"Yes, I'm fine, just a little tired," she replied, dredging up a smile for him. "It's been a long day."

Jonas looked unconvinced. "You're pale," he said, frowning as he examined her colorless cheeks. "And now that I think about it, you've been tired a lot lately." His eyes narrowed. "And you look unnaturally fragile. I think you should call your doctor and make an appointment to have a complete checkup."

"Jonas, I am—" Val caught herself in time. She had planned to call their friend, her obstetrician Milton Abramowitz, that coming Monday. Catching her breath, she went on, "I am fine."

"You'd better get plenty of rest while I'm gone," he ordered, drawing her into his embrace with a show of tenderness that brought fresh tears to her eyes. "Because if you're still pale and tired when I get home, I'll personally escort you to the doctor." He buried his face in her hair and murmured, "Is that understood?"

Val sniffed and managed a strangled-sounding laugh. "Yes, sir, Mr. Thorne, sir."

"I want you to crawl into bed as soon as I leave," he said. "And stay there for the weekend, if you feel like it."

"Jonas!" Val exclaimed, pulling back her head to stare at him. "I'm going with you to the airfield!"

Jonas shook his head. "Val, it's after four now. You're already overtired. If you go with me, it'll be at least six by the time you get home. I don't think..."

Val lifted her small chin in a defiant manner that was all too familiar to him. "I'm going with you, Jonas."

They drove through the hushed quiet of predawn, along streets empty except for an occasional car. There was more traffic on the highway, primarily tractor-trailers and delivery trucks. They didn't speak much; there was little left to say. Val began to miss Jonas even before they arrived at the small airstrip where Jonas rented hangar space for the Lear.

The others—Marge, Mary Beth and Jean-Paul—were already there, waiting beside Jean-Paul's elegant new Chrysler. Val heard the whine of the Lear's jets the moment Jonas brought the Lincoln to a stop alongside his son-in-law's car.

Stepping out of the vehicle, Val went directly to Mary Beth. The young woman looked as tired as Val felt.

"I sincerely hope Lynn will be all right," Val said, drawing the trembling girl into her arms. "And Mary Beth, try to get some sleep during the flight." Stepping back, Val smiled through her own tears. "Don't forget, you must take care of your father's—" she hesitated, then went on more strongly "—*our* grandchild."

"I'll be careful," Mary Beth promised, sniffing. "Thank you, Val."

"Come along, *chérie*," Jean-Paul murmured, slipping his arm around his wife's waist. "It's time to board." He turned to gaze solemnly at Val. "You take care of yourself, Valerie."

"I will." Val hugged Jean-Paul and Marge, then turned to Jonas. "And you take care of yourself."

"Come here," Jonas said, hauling her into his arms. He kissed her hard, but fast, then released her and quickly stepped back, as if afraid he'd never let her go if he didn't leave at once. "Drive carefully on your way home," he ordered, as he bent to pick up his valise. "Rest. I'll call you tomorrow." He made a face and shook his head. "Later today." He stared at her longingly for an instant, then abruptly swung away. "Be good," he called back softly as he strode toward the plane.

Val felt an ominous sensation of fear as she watched him walk away from her. It was strange, for she had never before been anxious about Jonas flying. But now oppressive fear was clutching at her throat.

The others had boarded, and Jonas was nearing the plane, when suddenly Val broke into a run. "Jonas!" she cried, running to him and launching herself against his reassuring strength.

His free arm caught her to him and she clung, hugging him fiercely. "What it is? What's wrong, darling?" he demanded, searching her tear-streaked face.

"Nothing." Val shook her head, not understanding herself. "Only please remember that I love you."

"I'll remember." Jonas's arm tightened compulsively, crushing her softness to him. His mouth covered hers in a deep kiss. "If you'll remember that I only adore you," he murmured, smiling as he raised his head.

"I'll remember," she promised, returning his smile, if a little tremulously.

And then Jonas was gone.

Val stood alone on the airstrip, straining her eyes until the jet's wing lights flickered and disappeared into the muted glow of dawn.

She slept badly. Although she had dropped onto the bed like a stone when she got back to the house, Val only dozed in fits and starts, waking suddenly each time with the shakes. Around noon she gave up trying to sleep and dragged herself from the bed. A shower didn't go very far toward reviving her body or her spirits.

Val spent the day prowling around the house, back and forth like some wild creature, caged and edgy. She occupied herself by glancing at the clock, then at whatever phone was closest, then at the clock again.

She was at a loss to account for or pinpoint the reason for her uneasiness. Jonas traveled often for business purposes, and was often gone for as long as a week. But although she had always missed him, she had never reacted to his absence in this panicky way.

Telling herself that she was being ridiculous didn't help. Assuring herself that she'd have heard something by then, if there had been any difficulty during the flight, didn't help, either. The unsettling sensation persisted, filling her mind with terrifying thoughts of the direst catastrophes imaginable.

When at last the phone did ring, Val jumped, startled by the sound she had waited all day to hear. Running to the instrument, she snatched the receiver from its cradle.

"Hello. Jonas?" she blurted out.

"Yes, love," Jonas replied, in a steady voice. "How are you?"

"I'm fine," Val lied. "How are *you*?"

"Bushed," he replied with a tired laugh. "It's been a very long day."

"How was the flight?"

"Uneventful. Mary Beth, Marge and Jean-Paul slept through most of it."

"But not you." It wasn't a question; Val knew her husband. "You should have."

"I dozed a little."

As I did. Val didn't offer that information. "I'm glad Mary Beth got some rest. I was concerned."

"So was I," he admitted. "But she's okay now that she's seen her mother."

Val shivered. "How is Lynn, Jonas?"

Jonas sighed. "She was banged up pretty badly. She was in surgery when we arrived." He sighed again.

"But she is conscious, or at least she was a short time ago when she spoke to Mary Beth. And the doctors are optimistic. They've downgraded her condition from critical to serious. But it'll be a while before she can travel."

Val felt a quiver of unease. "Travel?"

"Of course," Jonas replied. "We can't leave her here on her own. Neither Mary Beth nor Marge would have any rest if we did. So tomorrow—" he paused "—later today, I'm going to start making arrangements to fly her home as soon as her doctors give the okay for her to be moved."

"I understand." Val sighed in silent acceptance of what must be. "This means you're going to have to stay longer than the three or four days you'd planned on, doesn't it?"

"I'm afraid so." This time, Jonas's sigh was harsh with frustration. "Damn it, I miss you like hell already, and it hasn't even been twenty-four hours."

The endearingly familiar sound of him swearing made Val feel a little better. Enough to smile. "I miss you like hell, too," she confessed.

"I've noticed lately that you're beginning to curse pretty often, Mrs. T.," Jonas said in a low, intimate drawl.

"It's the company I keep," Val explained.

Jonas laughed, then yawned. "Sorry."

"You're tired. You'd better hang up and go to bed, Jonas," she said, hating the thought of losing the verbal contract with him.

"I don't want to hang up," he murmured. "I don't want to lose the closeness of the sound of your voice."

"I don't want to hang up, either."

"But I must, love. I'm falling asleep on my feet."

Val's eyes smarted, and her voice was unsteady with the threat of tears. "Good night, darling. I love you."

"I remember. And I only adore you." Jonas's tone was tender. "Good night, love. I'll call you tomorrow."

Sniffling, and chiding herself for being a fool, Val hung up the phone and went straight to bed—straight to sleep. She slept around the clock and woke shortly after dawn spread its pink and mauve glow over the summer landscape. Rested and refreshed, she stood at the window, watching the golden glitter of morning illuminate the terrain, wishing Jonas was beside her, yearning inside to share the wonder of it all with him.

But he wasn't there, and no amount of wishing could whisk him magically across thousands of miles to her side, Val told herself, turning away from the window. And pacing the length and breadth of the house, as she had yesterday, wouldn't change the situation either, she continued in the same self-chastising vein. She had work to do . . . the work she should have taken care of with dispatch the day before, instead of prowling aimlessly.

"Serves you right for not hiring one of the women the domestic service agency sent out," Val muttered to herself as she went into the shower.

"You could've hired any one of those women," she went on a few minutes later, as she stepped into her cleaning attire of jeans and a T-shirt. "They all had excellent references."

Throughout the morning, as she went briskly about her chores, Val kept the encroaching silence at bay with the sound of her own scolding voice.

"That last woman...what was her name? Oh, yes, Grace...mmm, Grace...Vining! That's it." Val snapped her fingers. "Grace Vining. She was very nice, the motherly type. I could use a motherly type right now." Val sighed and murmured, "I wonder if she's still available?" Deciding to call the agency in the morning, Val finished folding the last of the laundry.

Val read the Sunday paper while she methodically chewed and swallowed the salad she'd tossed together for lunch. Prince Valiant was in the midst of a battle; Mandrake had everything under control, and Hagar brought a reluctant smile to her lips. She was puzzling over Doonesbury when the phone rang.

Since she wasn't expecting Jonas to call until much later, Val took her time answering. She knew from the underlying note of tension in his first words that Jonas was angry about something.

"What's the matter?" Val asked after the initial exchange of greetings. "Why are you angry?"

"It's obvious, huh?"

"I can practically see your teeth grinding together," Val said. "Is it bad?"

"Not so much bad as annoying," he answered. "Our Lynn has made the headlines.

Val frowned. "Because of the accident?"

"Because of who she was with at the time of the accident," Jonas explained.

Val waited a moment, then when he wasn't forthcoming, she exclaimed, "Jonas! Who was she with?"

Jonas rattled off a name that Val immediately recognized, simply because it appeared in print with almost boring regularity. She sifted through her memory to recall what she had read about the man. Memory stirred and Val exhaled a sigh of impatience with Lynn. The man in question was handsome, held the title of *comte* or something, and was impoverished.... At least he had been before his marriage two years ago to the very wealthy and reputedly insanely jealous daughter of one of the wealthiest men in Europe. The man was also some ten or so years younger than Lynn.

"Oh boy," Val breathed.

"Exactly." Jonas swore.

"Was he badly injured?"

"Yes," Jonas answered. "But not as badly as Lynn. We didn't get the details concerning the crash until this afternoon, and only then through Jean-Paul." He paused, and Val could almost see him massaging the back of his neck, as he habitually did when he was angry and frustrated.

"Jonas, calm down," she murmured into the silence.

"Yeah, okay." His harsh sigh sang over the transatlantic connection. "Anyway, it turns out that they had just left Paris to return to the South of France, after having spent a few days' *holiday* together in a friend's château on the outskirts of Paris. He was driving...thus totaled the Porsche his wife gave him just last month for his thirtieth birthday.''

"This sounds like the scenario of a bad glitzy movie," Val observed.

"I wish to hell it was," Jonas retorted. "In her own inimitable way, Lynn has managed to create the juiciest scandal of the season. The newspapers are having a field day."

"Scandal sells."

"Tell me about it," he said in a dry tone. "And it'll probably get worse before it gets any better. The wife's outraged, and already making noises like..." Jonas hesitated, as if searching for a descriptive word.

"A wife?" Val interjected sweetly.

Jonas chuckled, and Val could hear the release of tension in the sound. "Purely theoretically, of course, but if it were me, would you make noises?"

"Of course not, darling," she purred. "I would very quietly kill you."

Jonas roared with laughter. "Love me that much, do you?" he asked when the laughter subsided.

"That much," Val confessed. "And more."

His laughter ceased, and was replaced by a low groan. "Oh, Val, what would I do without you?"

"Forget how to laugh?"

"Worse," he murmured. "I'd probably forget how to live."

"Jonas."

"Oh, hell." He groaned again. "I've got to get off this phone."

Val blinked. "Why?"

"Because I'm getting visions of you wearing a sexy black teddy."

"But I'm wearing faded jeans."

Jonas's voice grew low. "The tight ones?"

Were they? Frowning, Val looked down at herself. They were. "Yes, but how...?"

Jonas didn't let her finish. "I knew it. You look sexy wearing them, too."

Val absently slid her palm over her hip. "Do I?" She hardly recognized the sultry-sounding voice as her own.

"Mmm," Jonas murmured. "But you look even sexier not wearing them."

Her face grew warm, her limbs grew weak and her mind formed some erotic visions of him, too. "I miss you."

Jonas caught a quick breath. "I miss you, as well. And I want you... now. So you see, if I don't get off this phone, I'll be making love to you long-distance. And very likely melt the transcontinental wires in the process."

"Good night, Jonas," Val whispered. "I love you."

"I remember."

Val lived for the daily phone calls from Jonas through the days that followed. To fill the long hours between calls, she kept herself almost constantly occupied.

On Monday morning, Val made an appointment to see her obstetrician at the end of that week. Then she called the domestic service agency to inquire about the motherly-looking Grace Vining. On learning that Mrs. Vining was not only still available, but anxious to start working as soon as possible, Val asked the woman at the agency to send Grace right over.

Val liked Grace Vining even more after the second interview, and was prepared to hire her on the spot, if she would agree to one stipulation. Val had decided she would prefer a full-time, live-in housekeeper.

"Well, what do you say?" Val asked, after she finished showing Grace through the house and explaining what would be expected of her.

Grace Vining's rounded face creased with a wide smile. "I think you're the answer to all my prayers," she replied.

"In what way?" Val asked, intrigued.

The woman sighed. "It's a long story."

Val shrugged. "Okay, come out to the kitchen and we'll heat some soup or make a couple sandwiches. You can tell me your story over lunch."

Grace gaped at her. "But, I can't do that, Mrs. Thorne!" she exclaimed in obvious shock.

"Why not?" Val asked with a frown. "Do you have another appointment?"

"Well, no, but—" Grace shook her head "—you're my employer and all—"

"And my name's not Legree," Val interjected, motioning Grace to follow her as she headed for the kitchen. "It's not Mrs. Thorne, either. It's Val or Valerie," she said, shrugging her shoulders. "Whichever you prefer."

"Valerie's a beautiful name," Grace said, trailing into the kitchen after Val. "I'd like to call you that.... If you're positive it's all right?"

"I insist." Val tossed her a grin from over the top of the open refrigerator door. "Jonas calls me Valerie only when he's exasperated with me."

"Mr. Thorne?"

"Yes," Val said, pulling the makings for sandwiches from the fridge.

"Will Mr. Thorne be here for lunch?" Grace asked timidly.

"Oh, no." Val backed away from the fridge and shut the door with a nudge of her hip. "Jonas never comes home for lunch during the week. And he won't be here for dinner, either. At least not for a while. He's out of town and—" Val's words were buried by the other woman's exclamation.

"What!" Grace cried in astonishment. "You're all alone in this big house?"

"Well, yes, until Jonas comes home, but—" That was as far as she got before Grace again interrupted her.

"That settles it then." Drawing herself up to her full, impressive height, which was a good six inches taller than Val, Grace planted her hands on her ample hips. "I can't in good conscience allow you to remain alone in this house. With your permission, I'll move in this afternoon."

"And she did," Val finished after relating the tale to Jonas when he called that evening. She had taken the call on the phone in their bedroom and was lying on the bed, the phone balanced on her stomach.

"She sounds intimidating," Jonas said, laughing softly.

"She's a cream puff," Val replied, laughing with him. "And she cooks like a dream."

"Stir-fry?" Jonas asked with interest.

"No, but I promised to teach her how to make your favorite dishes."

"Oh, stop, I'm getting hungry," he groaned. "As good as it is, I'm tired of rich French food."

Val kicked off her shoes and rubbed the soles of her feet over the spread. "I'll stir-fry shrimp and vegetables for dinner for you your first night home."

"On my first night home, I seriously doubt I'll be thinking much about food," Jonas drawled.

"Oh, Jonas." Val's toes curled into the spread's nap.

"Valerie, stop that."

"Stop what?"

"Stop saying 'Oh, Jonas' in that soft, seductive voice," he ordered. "The memory of it kept me up most of last night."

Val giggled at his phrasing. "Really?"

"Valerie," his voice was low with warning, "change the subject."

"To what?"

"Hell, I don't know!" Jonas growled. "Yes, I do. Did Mrs. Vining ever get around to telling you her long story?"

"Yes."

"Is it boring?" he asked, hopefully.

Val sighed. "It's sad."

"Lay it on me. Maybe it'll put me to sleep."

Val smiled. "I know it's very late there, so I'll make it short. Then you can go to bed. To begin, Grace is alone. I don't mean that she merely lives alone, she is alone. As she put it, she and her husband were never blessed with children. And so they lived for each other. Only had a few close friends. He died last year. And since she's not old enough to collect social security, money's getting a little tight."

"You were right," Jonas murmured. "That is sad."

"Yes." Val sighed. "At any rate, Grace said she was hoping to secure a live-in position and sell her house." She paused, then murmured, "Oh, Jonas, she said she couldn't bear to live with all the memories in the house."

Jonas was quiet a while, then he said, "You did say her references are good?"

"Impeccable," Val replied.

"And do you like her?"

"Oh, yes. And I know you'll like her, too."

"Okay, now Grace has a new house to live in," Jonas said. "And we'll give her some new memories to live with."

Val's eyes were misty. "Thank you, darling."

"For what?" he asked gruffly.

"For being you." She sniffed; he heard her.

"I'm going to hang up now. I think maybe I'll sleep better knowing you're not alone in the house." His voice lowered to a whisper-soft caress. "Good night, adored one."

"Good night, Jonas. I love you."

"I remember."

With the advent of Grace to hold down the home front, Val decided to work full-time rather than half days in the office. She honestly enjoyed her work, and keeping busy staved off the loneliness that enveloped her during the long hours between calls from Jonas.

On Tuesday, Jonas told her the scandal over Lynn's accident was beginning to die down in the newspapers. Val breathed a sigh of relief. They didn't talk long because the transatlantic connection was bad.

The minute Val heard his voice on Wednesday, Val knew he'd had good news.

"Lynn was moved from the constant care unit into a private room this afternoon," he told her at once. "And her doctors said that if she continues to improve at the rate she has been, we might be able to bring her back to the States by the middle of next week."

"Jonas, that's wonderful!" Val exclaimed, suddenly needing to be held by him. "I miss you so much."

"I know, love. I miss you as much. But at least now I have hope of getting home sooner than I had believed possible when I arrived here."

"But, darling," Val said, bringing up a consideration that threatened her elation, "will Lynn be well enough to endure a flight of that length?"

The sound of his soft laughter reassured her before he uttered another word. "She will now. I've managed to hire a plane from a business associate of Edouard Barrès's. I've also retained a private nurse. Lynn, the nurse, Marge and Mary Beth will be returning to the States in it."

Though she was reassured by his explanation, Val was also confused. Of course she knew who Edouard Barrès was, for the Frenchman was not only an associate of Jonas's, but Jean-Paul's former employer, as well. What she didn't understand was why Jonas had found it necessary to hire another plane.

"Is there something wrong with the Lear, Jonas?" she asked, frowning as she realized that he hadn't included either his own name or that of Jean-Paul on the passenger list he had given to her.

"No," he answered. "Jean-Paul and I will be flying home in the Lear. But the plane I hired is a large executive jet, complete with a private bedroom. In a bed, sedated, with a trained professional in attendance, Lynn should have no difficulty making the trip."

"A bedroom, no less," Val murmured. "How tantalizingly decadent."

"Yeah," Jonas agreed. "It's a sight to behold. As a matter of fact, I'm thinking about buying one."

"Jonas Thorne!" Now Val could laugh again. "Are you considering membership in the Mile-High Club?"

"The idea has very erotic possibilities," Jonas responded in a low, sexy voice that sent a shower of tingles cascading down her spine. "Even though I must admit that I feel a mile high every time we make love in our bed on the ground."

"Why, Jonas," Val said in a teasing tone, "I do believe you're turning into a romantic."

"And if I don't soon get home to you," he returned in a soft growl, "I'm afraid I'll be turning into a raving sex-starved maniac."

Her flagging spirits bolstered both by Jonas's fervently expressed need for her and the expectation that he would be home in a week or so, Val cruised through her work on Thursday.

But her spirits plunged at the sound of rage in his voice when he called early that evening.

"It's hit the fan," Jonas snarled in tones of fury and outrage. "The scandal's been revived, and my name and photograph are plastered all over every newspaper and yellow journalism rag in Europe."

"But ... how?" Val was stunned. "Why?"

"I'll tell you how," he snapped. "Some overeager news hound became curious about my visits to the hospital. He did some digging, added one and one, and managed to come up with four."

Val shivered at the sound of his voice. Jonas in a cold rage was not a pretty sight. And Jonas was definitely in a cold rage; Val could almost feel the chill emanating from the telephone wire. "Four?" she repeated blankly. "Jonas, please calm down and explain. I don't understand."

"It's simple enough," Jonas said. "The news hound sniffed along the trail Lynn has left littered with discarded lovers and ex-husbands over the years until he discovered the very first of the bunch . . . yours truly. He then apparently did his homework on me and decided I was news."

Val winced. She knew how much Jonas disliked personal publicity. He painstakingly worked at keeping a low profile. She knew also that he absolutely detested notoriety. Furthermore, she was very much afraid she knew the answer to her next question, but asked it just the same. "And the four you mentioned. Where does that come in?"

His low laughter had the sound of a feral growl. "Just where you'd suspect. The newspaper stories are loaded with speculation that instead of a triangle here, there might be the possibility of a quadrangle."

"But that's not true!" Val cried indignantly.

"Calm down, sweetheart," Jonas murmured. "It probably won't amount to more than a three-day wonder. I just wanted to warn you in case it hit the gossip columns in the States."

Had Val been able to look dispassionately at the situation, she might have concluded that it was almost funny. The conversation had begun with her attempt to calm him down, and ended with him soothing her. But Val was beyond viewing the debacle objectively. Upset and worried about him, she revealed the depth of her emotion when she wished him goodnight.

"Please remember that I love you, Jonas," she whispered fiercely.

"I remember," he said, repeating his now habitual response. "Remembering that is what's keeping me going."

Val's spirits were dragging on the floor behind her when she left the office Friday morning to keep her appointment with her obstetrician. After a thorough examination, Milt Abramowitz offered his opinion that Val was, as she'd suspected, into her sixth week of pregnancy. To confirm his opinion, he had his nurse draw a blood sample for a pregnancy test.

Val spent the intervening hours in a fever of anxiety. When the doctor called later in the afternoon to inform her that the test results were positive, her lagging spirits took flight.

During the hours that followed the call from the doctor, Val became a dedicated clock-watcher. She couldn't wait to tell Jonas that within a few months of becoming a grandfather, he would become a father again.

It was only as the time drew nearer to his expected call that Val began to have second thoughts, admittedly selfish ones, about telling him over the phone. By telling him now, she'd be denying herself the thrill of seeing his expression, and of being swept into his arms and crushed to his chest in his exuberance. Besides, it was an event they should share, Val thought dreamily, when they could witness the joy shining in each other's eyes. It was not a moment to be squandered on a long-distance telephone call.

She would wait, Val decided, and hug the news secretly to her until Jonas came home. She almost dreaded his call, afraid her excitement might overrule her decision, so that she'd find herself blurting out the announcement to him.

The time for his call came, and passed. Another hour crawled by. Then another. As on the day he'd left, Val paced their bedroom, silently ordering the phone to ring. Where was Jonas? she asked herself countless times. Why didn't he call? Was he ill? Had an unexpected crisis arisen, a setback to Lynn's recovery?

Through the night and into the dawn, Val was plagued by fears, doubts and dozens of questions. She had no answers. She was exhausted but couldn't rest. Something was wrong, she knew. Something had to be wrong or Jonas would call.

The phone rang just after six-thirty. Pouncing on the instrument, Val snatched up the receiver. Her voice was expelled from her throat on a gasping sigh.

"Jonas?"

"No, *ma chère*."

"Jean-Paul?" Panic dug its claws into Val's chest. "Jean-Paul, why are you calling? Where is Jonas?" she demanded, inwardly fighting a need to shout.

A tired sigh whispered through the connecting wires, then Jean-Paul said softly, urgently, "Valerie, you must now be brave."

"Brave?" Val whispered around the fear gathering in her throat. "Why must I be brave? Jean-Paul!" Now she did shout. "Where is Jonas?"

"I wanted...had to call you before..." His voice cracked, then he went on in a strangled tone, "You'll soon be receiving official notification, but I felt I had to—"

The words "official notification" wrenched a scream from Val's heart. "Where is Jonas?"

"He's been kidnapped."

Kidnapped? Kidnapped! Val's mind whirled. Her thoughts spun crazily. Kidnapped? No. It was ludicrous! Jonas? Ridiculous. It was a mistake. That was it! Someone had made a dreadful mistake. Jonas had not been kidnapped. Prominent men got kidnapped. Distinguished men, recognizable because their names and photographs were frequently seen in the newspa—

Val's thoughts ground to a sudden stop. Names and photographs. Newspapers. Jonas.

"...Valerie, Valerie, are you there? Do you hear me? Valerie, answer me!"

Jean-Paul's loud imploring voice crashed through the stunned horror gripping Val's mind. "Jean-Paul, when did this happen?" she cried. "How did this happen?"

"He was...taken as he was leaving the hospital this morning. Witnesses said that three men grabbed him and flung him into a waiting car. The car...got away."

"Taken?" she repeated in a voice that was barely there. "Grabbed? Flung?"

"Valerie, I swear to you that every effort possible is being made to apprehend the kidnappers," Jean-Paul said reassuringly. "Not an avenue will be overlooked in the effort to get Jonas back safely."

Val was beyond being reassured; she was in a state of abject terror. After Jean-Paul said he must hang up, she replaced the receiver, then sat on the edge of the bed, waiting for the phone to ring again, dreading the sound.

Official notification duly came, along with more words of assurance. Val heard and responded to the disembodied voice, while inside her head she screamed his name in agony.

Jonas.

When the initial shock wore off, Val took herself to task. Falling apart would not help Jonas, she told herself. He would be found and returned to her, she assured herself. Val determined that when Jonas was returned, it would not be to find either his wife or his business in a shambles.

Val asked questions of the authorities. She received evasive answers until Jean-Paul and the others came home a week later. It was some time before Val had an opportunity to talk to Jean-Paul in private. Mary Beth was a frightened wreck; Lynn had had a relapse; Marge had aged ten years.

"I want to know everything that you know," Val said to Jean-Paul when they were finally alone. "The authorities can't or won't tell me anything."

Faced with her defiantly lifted chin, Jean-Paul sighed. "All I've been able to garner from friends is that the authorities suspect the kidnappers were from Central America and that they fear he has been taken there."

Central America. Val fought a new, insidious fear. There was so much turmoil in some of the Central American countries. She had read accounts of terrible atrocities....

With sheer willpower, Val controlled her rioting imagination. She absolutely refused to fall apart. But Val did falter a little. "What do they want?" she cried. "They can have anything. They can have everything! If they'll only let Jonas go, set him free."

"As far as I know, no demands have yet been made," Jean-Paul said. He hesitated, then added with a Gallic shrug, "Valerie, I fear you must prepare yourself."

Val's heart thumped. "What do you mean?" she asked in a dry croak. "Prepare myself for what?"

Jean-Paul gripped her by her shoulders to support her trembling body. "I'm afraid, *ma petite*, that when demands are made, they will be political in nature, not financial." He paused again, as if gathering fortitude before continuing. "Valerie, you know the prevailing sentiment in this country about granting concessions of that sort."

Val broke then. Sobbing, she collapsed against Jean-Paul. Cradling her in his arms in much the same way he had during his brother's funeral five years before, he let her cry until the wracking sobs dwindled. Stroking her hair, he comforted her.

"We must be strong, you and I, *ma mignonne*." He smiled when she raised her tear-drenched eyes to his. "We must be strong for Jonas, and for his family, because we love him." Jean-Paul's eyes were suspiciously bright. "And because he would wish us to be strong and responsible."

Recalling her own assessment of Jonas's sense of responsibility the morning he had left for France, Val nodded her head. "Yes," she agreed softly. "Jonas would want that."

Gaunt and silent, and to all appearances docile and resigned, Jonas stood in the midst of his captors. Head hanging in apparent exhaustion, his expression blank, he listened to the agitated discussion between the five kidnappers, straining to catch a word he understood in the rapid-fire Spanish.

Jonas was in fact exhausted. He was also hungry, thirsty and filthy. But, though his attitude of weary acceptance didn't reveal it, more than anything else Jonas was furious.

The anger had begun simmering inside him soon after he regained consciousness. Initially he'd felt confused. He was in a plane, a rather decrepit prop plane. And he was securely bound at the wrists and ankles. A throbbing pain at the back of his head triggered Jonas's memory.

Jonas recalled the sharp suspicion he'd felt when four men had casually encircled him as he was leaving the hospital. Then, when he'd tried to step between two of them, his arms had been grasped on either side. Jonas remembered demanding an explanation an instant before a brutal blow to his head knocked him out cold.

Ignoring the thumping ache resulting from the blow, Jonas glanced around the shabby interior of the flying rattletrap. He was alone in the compartment. He had remained alone until a few minutes prior to landing.

At first, asking questions and demanding to know where he was being taken, Jonas had resisted being removed from the plane. All his efforts gained him were more brutal blows to the body and the verbal abuse of an angry spate of Spanish curses.

Jonas had not reached the pinnacle of success by being stupid. Deciding to bide his time and save wear and tear on his hide, at least until he could figure out where he was, he gave every appearance of being cowed. But inside him, simmering anger had grown into cold rage.

By Jonas's reckoning, he had now been in captivity nearly six full weeks. He had attempted to escape twice. He had been beaten and starved for his trouble. Having overheard mention of some city names, Jonas speculated that the plane had landed somewhere in South America and that he had been transported north into Central America. Intellect and reason told him that his ransom price was probably political in nature. Reason also told Jonas that unless he could pull off an escape, he was probably one dead bastard.

Now, after six weeks of moving at night from one crummy shack to another, Jonas knew something was about to happen. He and his five watchdogs had been in their current location for over a week. It was not the

Trump Plaza. Constructed primarily of sheets of rusting metal and wishful thinking, the place was a pigsty. Other than a single water pipe, there was no indoor plumbing.

An hour before, two men had joined their party of six. The discussion had been raging ever since. From the few words Jonas had been able to pick up, he knew something was going on. What he hadn't been able to figure out was whether that something was a deal or a raid. But whatever it was, it had sure managed to excite his captors and their two visitors. Every one of Jonas's senses was alert, quivering with an urgency for flight. It was now or never. Raising his head, Jonas added his voice to the babble of the others. He knew that at least two of the men understood English.

"Hey, I've got to relieve myself. Are one of you clowns going to take me out, or do I do my business in here?" He curled his lips into a sneer as he glanced around disdainfully. "Not that it'd make much difference in this cesspool."

As he'd expected, Jonas was rewarded for his sarcasm with a backhand rap across the face from the man nearest to him. But as he had hoped, the man snarled an order to one of the others to take Jonas to the "facility."

The other man made a gesture with the Uzi that was cradled in the crook of one arm and, head meekly lowered, Jonas preceded him from the shack.

The "facility" was located at the edge of a thicket, some distance behind the shack. The reason for the distance became apparent yards before reaching the three-foot-wide trench. The stench was awful.

With the Uzi poking him in the back, Jonas held his breath and stepped to the edge of the trench. Before he was completely finished, the thug behind him gave Jonas a shove with the butt of the gun.

Cursing the man viciously, Jonas twisted and went sprawling backward into the filth in the trench. He heard the man laugh sadistically—an instant before an earsplitting explosion shook the earth and plunged him into unconsciousness.

The weeks slipped by. Two became four, then five, then six. Holding onto hope for all she was worth, Val persevered. She lost weight, but hung on. She told no one about her pregnancy.

Between them, Val and Jean-Paul soothed, encouraged, and literally held everything and everyone together... Jonas's family as well as his business and employees.

On the second day of the seventh week, Val got home from work to find two men waiting for her. At the sight of Grace's pale face, Val began to tremble. The men introduced themselves and proffered official-looking identification for her inspection. Feeling the world crashing in on her, Val swallowed convulsively as the older man began to speak.

"Mrs. Thorne, I regret that I must inform you of the death of your husband, Mr. Jonas Thorne." He held out a small manila envelope, which she hadn't noticed at first. "I further regret that these two per-

sonal possessions of your husband's are all that we
found at the scene of the devas—"

"No." Val's whisper silenced the man; the scream
inside her head silenced her consciousness.

Jonas!

Chapter Nine

Val fought through the last clinging webs of slumber. Confusion blurred the line between sleep and consciousness. A frown tugging her brows together, she blinked and glanced around the room.

Long fingers of late-afternoon sunlight speared through the filmy window curtains, creating patterns of gold and shadow on the opposite wall.

What time was it? Val wondered, striving for complete awareness. Late afternoon? Early evening? Shifting her head on the pillow, she stared at the bedside clock. Six thirty-four? What was she doing in bed at six thirty-four in the evening?

Reality returned with sudden clarity, piercing the

numbness, restoring memory, stripping away the protective buffer that desensitized her mental anguish.

Jonas!

Val's thinking kicked into gear.

Those two official-looking men had said Jonas was... No, it wasn't true; it couldn't be true. Jonas couldn't be... But they had identification, and it looked genuine. They had said they were from some federal department. They had said Jonas was... They had brought a small tan envelope that held his personal possessions. No, it could not be true....

Val's eyes were now wide. Her gaze darted around the room, searching for a solid point of reference.

The mental wheels started to spin, and flung Val back seven weeks in time.

The bedroom! Of course! That was it. She had been pacing the bedroom, frantic with worry, waiting for Jonas to call. The last she remembered it was sunrise. She hadn't slept all night. That explained why she was in bed at six thirty-four in the evening. Exhausted, she must have finally fallen asleep, slept straight through the day. That was it. Had Jonas called? Had she missed Jonas's call?

Something stripped the gears, sending a shudder from Val's skull to her heels. Her thoughts stopped for a breath-catching instant. When her mind cranked up again, the rhythm was normal, unwinding regulated impulses of lucid thought.

Jonas hadn't called at all. Jean-Paul had called. And it had not been earlier that morning. The call from Jean-Paul had come seven weeks ago.

Jonas was dead. He would never call again.

"No!" Val sprang up and off the bed as the denial burst from her aching throat. Nausea invaded her stomach, her head whirled, darkness closed in on her and she flailed her arms around for something to hold on to.

There was nothing there. Val went down. She heard her body thud onto the cushioning carpet, felt a jolt of pain, and responded with a startled cry.

Val was pushing herself into a sitting position when the bedroom door was flung open.

"Mon Dieu!" Jean-Paul exclaimed, bursting into the room, Grace at his heels. "Valerie, what has happened?" he asked dropping to one knee beside her.

Raising a shaking hand, Val pushed her heavy, disheveled hair from her face. "I—I fell," she said in vague astonishment. "I must have gotten up too fast."

Grace bustled to her other side. "Are you all right?" she asked anxiously.

Her eyes dazed, Val glanced from one to the other. "Yes, I think so," she began, then her eyes flew wide and she cried, "Oh, my Lord! The baby!"

"Baby?" Jean-Paul repeated, frowning. "What baby? My baby? Mary Beth's baby?"

"I knew it!" Grace exclaimed.

Jean-Paul shot a blank look at the older woman. "I don't understand. What did you know?"

Val answered his question. "I'm pregnant." Swallowing convulsively, she gripped his arm. "Jean-Paul, please, will you call Dr. Abramowitz? I lost my first baby due to a fall. Dear God, I can't lose this one!"

After an instant of shocked stillness, Jean-Paul took command of the situation like a man who had been tutored by a dynamo...which he had been, of course. Scooping Val into his arms, he barked an order to Grace as he strode to the door. "I'm taking Valerie to the hospital. Call Dr. Abramowitz and ask him to meet us there."

The rain revived Jonas. Slowly he came to his senses. Through the fog he could feel a stabbing pain in the back of his head. As if echoing its pounding roar inside his skull, thunder rumbled overhead. The rain came down in torrents.

Where was he? Jonas winced; it hurt to think. Come to that, it hurt to breathe. Stifling a groan, he opened his eyes. He had to blink several times to clear his vision. The sight that met his gaze brought a frown to his brow.

"What the hell!"

There was a man lying above him, sprawled over what appeared to be the outer edges of a trough. Less than six inches separated the man's body from Jonas.

Startled, Jonas moved, intending to ease himself from beneath the man. Another groan escaped his throat as his head scraped against something hard. Rockets of pain exploded. Closing his eyes, Jonas drew in great gasping breaths. Then he gagged and his stomach heaved, protesting against the stench in the air. Ignoring the pounding in his head, he scrambled backward. It was only after he was clear of the other man that Jonas realized that his own head had been lying on a large rock. The pain he was suffering gave ample proof that his head had not struck the unlikely pillow gently. Dismissing the questions this realization activated, he heaved himself up and over the edge of the trough.

He was exhausted, but he was out of that disgusting hole. Lying on his back, Jonas closed his eyes and welcomed the cleansing beat of the rain against his filthy body. When the throbbing in his head subsided, and his breathing slowed to a near-normal rate, he carefully pushed himself up and opened his eyes once more.

Where was he? The question reverberated in Jonas's mind as his astonished eyes absorbed the scene of utter devastation around him. The area looked like a battlefield—a bombed-out battlefield. Twisted and burned pieces of debris cluttered the landscape. Wondering what the pieces used to be, Jonas shifted his gaze to the man lying suspended over the trench. The man's back was gone, as if literally torn away by a blast of enormous proportions.

Bile gushed into his throat. What in heaven's name had happened here? Jonas wondered sickly. And what was he doing here, wherever "here" might be? The questions were followed by another consideration, one that caused him to break into a cold sweat.

Who was he?

Sitting beside a stinking waste trench in the pouring rain, Jonas raked his mind for a memory... any memory. He found none. For an instant, stark terror gripped him. From the destruction around him, he appeared to be in the middle of a war zone, and he didn't know who he was, where he was, or where he belonged.

War zone. The thought unlocked the grip of fear on his mind. Immediately his senses picked up the muted sounds of movement in the distance. He had to get away.

Jonas jackknifed to his feet. His head reeled. Gritting his teeth, he fought back the wave of darkness that threatened to wash over him until his equilibrium was restored. When the world was again in focus, he began to move. Without a backward glance at the scene of destruction, he slipped into the dense thicket of evergreen and deciduous trees surrounding the leveled compound.

Jonas struggled through the thick growth of foliage until he felt far enough away to avoid detection. Then, standing exposed in a tiny clearing, he stripped to the skin and let the pouring rain sluice the filth from his body. When he felt relatively clean, he spread out his clothes and beat them clean with a stout stick. By the time he was satisfied with the combined efforts of the pouring rain and the pounding of the stick, he was exhausted and breathing heavily. Pulling on the sodden garments, he methodically searched the clothing for some form of identification. There was nothing— no billfold, no papers, no money, no clues at all. Shoulders drooping in weariness and resignation, he moved back into the undergrowth in search of a place to rest.

The best Jonas could find was a tall, full, broad-leafed plant. It afforded some protection from the heavy rain and concealed his curled-up body from casual observation. Jonas went to sleep hungry, but he was able to slake his thirst by catching rainwater in his cupped hands.

When Jonas awoke the sun was shining. It was early and already hot and humid. Water dripped from every tree and plant. Jonas didn't mind the dripping water, the heat or the humidity. He was famished, he still felt excessively tired, but the thumping inside his head had subsided to a dull ache. After standing and testing his strength, Jonas decided he'd survive until he found something to eat.

Since he had no idea who he was, where he was, or where he came from, Jonas had no idea where he was going. Yet strangely, intuition or instinct—some inner something—urged him to move in a northerly direction. Judging direction by the position of the sun, he headed north without question or doubt.

Val half sat, half reclined against plumped pillows in the large bed. A brown envelope lay on her lap. Her small hand clutched the contents of the envelope close to her breast. Jean-Paul and Mary Beth were seated in the room's two easy chairs, which had been moved close to the bed. Jean-Paul looked grim; Mary Beth was weeping softly.

At Val's insistence, but against his better judgment, Milton Abramowitz had released her from the hospital after twenty-odd hours of close observation.

He had urged her to stay, for although she had suffered no injuries from her fall, Val was in a deep state of emotional shock and depression. Unable to keep her in the hospital against her will, the doctor had relented on condition that Val have complete bed rest at home.

"It's true, isn't it?" Val said, her expression stark with the knowledge she could no longer deny. "Jonas really is dead, isn't he?"

"Yes, *ma chèrie*," Jean-Paul murmured, tightening the grip of his hand around his wife's cold fingers. "I'm afraid we must accept the truth that Jonas is dead. The information was released this morning. It is the headline story in all the afternoon newspapers."

"How...?" Val's voice failed, and she had to draw a breath before continuing. "How did he die? Was he murdered?"

Jean-Paul winced at the harsh sound of pain in her voice. His hand gripped Mary Beth's trembling fingers. "Valerie, *ma petite*, believe me, you do not want to hear." He heaved a sigh. "It is an ugly story."

Val caught her breath, but determination was written on her pale face. "No, I don't want to hear about it," she said struggling for control. "But don't you understand that I must hear, Jean-Paul? I must know, or else I'll never be able to believe, accept...." Once again her voice failed. The expression in Val's eyes pleaded for understanding and compliance.

Sitting forward in her chair, Mary Beth supported Val's insistence in a quivering plea of her own. "Val's right, Jean-Paul. I keep thinking it's all a mistake, that any minute the phone will ring and—'' she sobbed ''—and it'll be Daddy, telling us it was all a horrible mistake.'' Shudders rippled through her body.

Releasing her hand, Jean-Paul put his arm around her violently shaking shoulders and drew her close to the protective strength of his own trembling body. "All right,'' he said on a sigh, relenting. "I will be brief. But perhaps I should relate to you what I was told unofficially by friends. It seems that Jonas was kidnapped by one of the newer, relatively small but apparently violent takeover groups to appear on the scene in an already strife-torn country in Central America. My informants told me the group consists mainly of malcontents and ex-mercenaries looking for the main chance.''

''But what did these men hope to gain by kidnapping Jonas?'' Val asked in a strained voice.

Jean-Paul moved his shoulders in a weary shrug. "Who knows? Recognition, political leverage...it's anyone's guess.'' His sigh conveyed a sense of futility. "At any rate, the authorities here learned that Jonas was being held in a remote, heavily forested area and a rescue mission was activated. But meanwhile there was apparently friction within the group itself. I was given no details. All I know is that when the rescue contingent arrived at the location, they found complete and utter devastation. The place had been leveled, destroyed by bombing.'' He paused, as if dreading the need to continue.

Val sat as if frozen. Her lips barely moved as she prompted him. "Go on, finish it."

Jean-Paul shut his eyes. When he opened them again, they were dark, shadowed by horror. "All the rescue team found in their search through the debris were bits and pieces, Valerie."

Val flinched, as if from a hard physical blow. Jean-Paul's free hand shot out to steady her. Her control shattered. "So this is all I'm to have of him?" Val cried in anguished protest. Lowering her hand, she opened her fingers and stared at the two articles in her palm. "This is all that's left of my husband?"

"And my father," Mary Beth whimpered, shuddering as a heart-wrenching sob was torn from her throat.

Springing from his chair, Jean-Paul gently drew his sobbing wife into his arms, consoling her with endearments murmured in French.

Tears running unheeded down her face, Val stared at the two objects in her hand. The metal was twisted and the edges blurred by melting from intense heat, yet the objects were identifiable as Jonas's wedding ring and the watch Val had purchased for him in San Francisco for his birthday. Barely discernible, Val could still make out the inscription she'd had etched on the back of the watch.

"This isn't fair!" Val cried, closing her fingers and once more clutching her hand close to her breast. "It just isn't fair! Is this what I'm to show Jonas's child?" she demanded. "And all because of some demented, self-styled would-be rulers? Jean-Paul, Jonas never

even knew that he was going to be a father again!"
Sliding down on the bed, she curled into a ball and
gave way to uncontrollable sobs.

His expression revealing his sense of helplessness in
the face of two grief-stricken women, Jean-Paul
heaved a sigh of relief when Grace came bustling into
the room. "You take care of your little lady. Mr.
DeBron," she said softly. "I'll take care of Valerie."

In truth, there was very little anyone could do to
care for Valerie, other than see to her obvious physical needs. Desolate and inconsolable, Val withdrew
into herself. She ate only enough to sustain the life and
health of her child. She slept fitfully. She didn't leave
the bedroom and rarely left her bed. Jonas was dead.
Val's instinct for survival had died with him. She no
longer wished to live.

Condolences poured in after Jonas's death was re-
ported in the newspapers. The employees of the firm
were devastated by the news. The evidence of the high
esteem in which Jonas had been held by scores of
people all over the world, as well as in the States, did
not surprise Valerie, but it did little to alleviate her remorse or ease her sense of loss.

Cloistered in the bedroom she had shared with
Jonas, existing primarily on her memories of him, Val
locked out the rest of the world. In much the same way
as she had after the death of her fiancé, Jean-Paul's
brother, Etienne, four and a half years before, Val
closed herself off from everyone. Only this time it was
worse, much worse. Etienne had been Val's first love,
and with his loss, she had suffered the death of love's

young dream. Losing Jonas was a deeper anguish, like losing the most vital part of herself.

Val was bitter and she was angry. In an agony of grief, she ranted in silent fury against a fate so cruel as to rob her of newfound happiness, not once but twice.

With the loss of Jonas, Val relived their time together over and over in her mind, especially their time since their reconciliation in San Francisco. Listening intently to the echo of Jonas's voice, Val was deaf to the reasoning of other, living voices. Jean-Paul could not reach her. Mary Beth could not reach her. Marge could not reach her. Not even Janet could get through to Val, as she had in Paris over three years before.

To all intents and purposes Valerie had abdicated from life, shutting out the people who loved her. Inside her head, she heard and wept with the echoing sound of Jonas's whispering voice.

I remember. I remember. I remember....

Because of his compelling inner determination to trek in a northerly direction, it took Jonas only two months to get across the border into Mexico. It would have taken him longer, if it hadn't been for the occasional rides he picked up from friendly farmers along the way. Jonas would probably also have faced starvation, if it hadn't been for the food provided by those same farmers. At other times, Jonas survived by applying the keen intelligence that had enabled him to work his way up from the status of penniless orphan to the ownership of one of the most prestigious electronics firms in the world.

Though his memory of past events was gone, Jonas possessed common sense, and knew that if he was apprehended without identification papers he could be in big trouble. Whenever possible, he traveled parallel to guiding roads, not close enough to be observed by any passing traffic, yet near enough to recognize the farm vehicles. He ate off the land, availing himself of a tiny portion of the farmers' crops of fruits and vegetables.

During the first month, the going was arduous because of the mountainous terrain. During the second month, the going was arduous because, skirting the mountains, he traveled through a section of the dense rain forest. Jonas grew gaunt, and since he was without the luxury of a razor or even a pocketknife, he grew a beard, which surprisingly came out red, liberally peppered with gray. When his clothes deteriorated to the point of falling in shreds from his thin body, Jonas stole others, which seldom fitted but at least covered and protected him.

The urge inside him to keep moving northward inexplicably grew stronger after he crossed the border into Mexico. Following that inner directive, he continued along the course he had intuitively adopted, avoiding towns and villages, eating off the land where possible, and accepting help from farmers whenever it was offered.

Dodging, wary and cautious, it took Jonas another month and a half to reach the Mexico-Texas border. He crossed the line somewhere between Nuevo Laredo and Rio Bravo exactly as many others had before him, by getting his back wet.

When he crawled out of the water onto United States soil, Jonas drew a deep breath of relief. He still didn't know who he was, where he belonged, or where his inner urge was leading him. But deep inside, Jonas was certain of one thing. He knew he was in his own country. Armed with that knowledge, Jonas felt he could endure anything.

Val awoke with a start in the middle of a cold night in early November. Something had wakened her. But what? A dream? A sound? What? She frowned into the darkness. A moment passed, quiet, still, then Val's frown changed to a wide-eyed expression of sheer wonder.

She had been awakened by the one sensation powerful enough to rouse her from her lethargy—the tiny flutter of quickening life inside her body.

Her baby had moved! Jonas's child was alive and making his presence felt within her womb. Tears rushed to Val's eyes as she carefully slid her palm over her gently mounded belly. Motionless, barely breathing, she waited.

The flutter came again, stronger, more definite. Trembling, Val whispered into the shadowed room.

"Jonas, our baby, the child of our love is alive." A short bubble of laughter burst from her throat as the sensation was repeated. "Darling, I can feel him stretching his tiny limbs inside my body."

Her hand pressed protectively over her abdomen, Val shuddered as sobs wrenched from her throat. She had often given way to her tears during the past two months, but this time Val wept tears of healing. Within minutes she was laughing and crying at the same time. Her baby had moved, and in so doing had restored to Val the desire to live.

Val did not go back to sleep. Lying in the darkness, she reviewed the self-indulgence of the past two months and found herself wanting. In retrospect, she realized that she had been so self-absorbed, so steeped in self-pity that she had barely noticed the passage of time, had been oblivious of the fact that the heat of summer had surrendered to the crisp air of autumn. Only now was she prepared to acknowledge the pain, suffering and anxiety of those around her, including those most important to Jonas . . . his family.

Jonas would not be proud of her, Val admitted to herself. Nor would he be pleased by her willful repudiation of life. Jonas had felt disdain for quitters, especially those who in his own words copped out on life.

Jonas Thorne had been more than a fighter in the battle of life; he had been a genuine scrapper. The insight gave Val's depleted spirits a shot of determination. Lifting her small chin, she whispered once more into the darkened room.

"From here on, my love, I promise that I will be a scrapper, too. Your responsibilities will be my responsibilities. And I will do more than fight and scrap for the welfare of our child; I will live for him."

Her energy renewed, Val waited impatiently for the dawn. Not for an instant did she doubt that the child quickening with life inside her was a son.

Jonas spent over ten weeks in Texas. Not a glimmer of his memory had returned. But, if nothing else, since entering the States he now knew the date, month and year. He also knew the value of a dollar. That particular bit of knowledge amused him, considering the fact that he didn't possess as much as a dime.

Though the urge to keep moving north grew stronger with each passing day, and he continued to obey that urge, he progressed with calculated slowness. He was exhausted, he was undernourished, he was emaciated, and he knew it. He also knew somehow that though the fall weather was mild in the Southwest, it would be growing cold in the Northeast.

Reason cautioned him to bide his time in the temperate climate before attempting to face the biting onset of winter to the north. He needed rest. He needed food. He needed to rebuild his flagging strength.

Without funds, and looking like a wild man who had just fought his way through a wilderness—which, in effect, he had—Jonas had few options available for seeing to his needs. The most obvious of those options was to seek assistance at the shelters that were operated for and utilized by the street people—the homeless, the rejected, the dropouts.

Drifting in a northeasterly direction, Jonas stayed a few days, at times an entire week, in small towns along his route.

In one of the first of those towns, Jonas was offered a bath by a kind but harried-looking man who was hard-pressed to keep from wrinkling his nose in distaste. Jonas accepted the offer with controlled eagerness. The man had shown him to the bathroom, then hurried away, telling Jonas he'd bring clean clothes for him to wear. The room had held a commode and an old, claw-footed, rust-stained porcelain tub. Jonas had luxuriated in both of the conveniences.

Jonas never knew what happened to the rags he'd torn from his skinny body, but then he didn't particularly want to know. The clothes the overworked man brought to him were used but had been well cared for and, luxury of luxuries, they fitted, as did the previously worn but still serviceable shoes and socks the man had placed atop the folded garments.

When he was clean and decently attired, Jonas was provided with a hot meal and his first cup of steaming coffee. Grateful for the man's kindness, Jonas savored every bite of food and every sip of the coffee. When he had finished eating, Jonas asked the man if there was some work he could do as a measure of repayment for the bath, clothing and food. Grateful for the offer of help in the understaffed shelter, the man assigned him the job of washing dishes.

Staggering with exhaustion, but determined, Jonas stood for some four hours washing and drying the seemingly never ending flow of dishes the man brought to him.

"You got a name, mister?" the man asked when he entered the large kitchen with the last load of dirty dishes.

Jonas hesitated, then spoke the first name to spring into his mind. "John. The name's John."

The man smiled with wry acceptance. "Isn't everybody's?" Not waiting or expecting a response, he thrust out his hand. "Mine's Hopkins, Ben Hopkins, and I appreciate the help. Flu goin' around and we're shorthanded." He indicated a shed off the back of the kitchen. "There's a cot in there. You can flop for the night if you've no place else to go."

"Thanks, Ben." Jonas strove to keep his voice steady; he nearly made it. "I have someplace to go, but I'm just too damned tired to keep moving."

Ben studied Jonas's eyes for several seconds, then nodded. "If you don't mind working, you can stay a few days, eat, rest up."

Jonas's throat worked and his voice cracked. "I don't mind working, and I appreciate the offer. Thanks again."

Ben shrugged and headed for the doorway. "It's nothing. Like I said, we're shorthanded."

Jonas stayed at the shelter until one of the volunteers returned to duty five days later. It was to be the first of many shelters. He was always given food, and sometimes a cot or pallet to sleep on, but either way, Jonas always insisted on doing some sort of work in payment for the bounty received.

Ten weeks after entering Texas, Jonas crossed the state line into Louisiana. With his constant moving and working, Jonas hadn't managed to gain any weight, but his strength was returning. He was ready to move on, still heading north.

Val was tired. Resting her head against the plush seat back, she closed her eyes and tried to relax. Being driven home from the office was a new experience for her; Val had always driven herself. But it had begun snowing around noon, and by quitting time the driving was hazardous. Not wanting to take unnecessary chances in her advanced state of pregnancy, Val had placed a call to the company garage to ask Lyle Magesjski to drive her home.

"Sure thing, Mrs. Thorne," Lyle had said, as if genuinely pleased to be of service. "Tell me what time you'll be ready to leave, and I'll be at the door."

Lyle had been with Jonas for fifteen years. He'd been devoted to him. Now his devotion had been extended to Valerie.

Jonas.

Listening to the swish of the windshield wipers, Val sighed and conjured up an image of Jonas's strong, chiseled face. Late-winter snowstorm notwithstanding, it was almost spring. Her projected due date was only two weeks away. It was six months since she had received notification of Jonas's death. Four months had passed since she had awakened to the flutter of life inside her. Val's mouth curved into a tender smile.

Jonas's child now at times appeared determined to kick and punch his way out of her body.

She missed Jonas terribly. There were moments when Val felt certain she could not bear to go on one second longer weighed down by the knowledge that she would never see her husband again. Her sense of loss, her anguish, had not lessened with the passing days and weeks and months. Val merely kept the loss, the anguish to herself, hidden behind the charge she'd assumed to care for his family and for the business Jonas had worked so very hard to make succeed.

Jonas had a granddaughter he would never see. Two months before, Mary Beth had given birth to a fiery red, squalling, beautiful baby girl. The baby was born with Jean-Paul's dark hair and coloring and her mother's bright blue eyes.

Val adored the baby and had secretly vowed to protect the heritage of both Jonas's granddaughter and that of his own child.

With inner amusement, Val recalled the expressions of skepticism and doubt she'd received when she had returned to the office the day after she had felt her baby's first tentative movements. Everyone, from Jean-Paul to Charlie to Janet and straight down the line of employees and family had been sympathetic; some, like Janet and Marge, even encouraging. But none of them believed she could actually run the company in Jonas's stead.

Satisfaction replaced her amusement as Val reflected on her own rather amazing accomplishments of the previous four months. She had moved into his office with bold decisiveness. By working night and day, she had studied and learned until she knew the business inside and out and even sideways. While certain that no one could replace, let alone match Jonas's genius, Val knew he had hired brilliant electronic engineers who, with the proper support and leadership, were fully capable of maintaining the company's excellent position.

Val had taken control, and she had succeeded. She was tired, but she had grown used to being tired. And on a snowy evening in mid-March, she was aching for Jonas. She knew she would never grow used to the ache. She would live with it. Val had no choice. She had his family, even Lynn who, upon full recovery from her injuries, had wisely decided to take her mother's advice to grow up, and was proving to be a surprisingly effective grandmother. Val had his company, whose employees had rallied around her to a man . . . and woman. And before too long, Val would have a part of Jonas himself, in the form of the child they had conceived in love.

Val was content . . . or as content as possible while silently screaming in agony.

Chapter Ten

Two days after the official arrival of spring, Val sat propped up in a hospital bed, cradling her own spring arrival in her arms. Tears ran down her cheeks as she gazed into the face of Jonas's son and tiny image.

Her labor had been long and hard, but the advent of the infant Val had already named Jonas had been worth every minute of the pain it had involved.

"The likeness is incredible," Jean-Paul observed, staring in astonishment at the baby.

"Yes." Glancing up, Val smiled through her tears. "Isn't it wonderful?"

"It's . . . almost like having Dad back," Mary Beth murmured, reaching out to stroke a trembling finger over one downy pink cheek.

Val shifted her tear-bright violet eyes to the younger woman. "A part of him," she agreed softly.

"And we'll always have that part of him, won't we?" Mary Beth raised eyes shining with hope and happiness. "As long as we have baby Jonas, we'll have a living part of Dad."

Cradling the baby in one arm, Val reached out to grasp Mary Beth's hand. "Yes, we'll always have a living memory of your father... of Jonas."

Later that night, as Val coaxed her son to suckle nourishment from her breast, she stared into his new, yet endearingly familiar face and made a silent vow.

I remember, Jonas. I'll always remember.

The urge was stronger now inside Jonas, so strong that at times he had to fight against an overwhelming need to run.

Where did the inner pressure want him to run to?

The question was beginning to torment him. The urge had expanded in time with his slow movement north.

Jonas had planned to spend the winter months in the warmer climate of the southern states, but the urge persisted, overriding his common sense. Unable to rest after a stop of more than a few days in any one place, Jonas kept moving north, ever north.

He took refuge in shelters, and as he had in Texas, Jonas repaid every kindness with whatever work needed doing. He mopped floors, he washed dishes, he cleaned toilets. No task was too menial or beneath his dignity. The rewards of his labor were sustenance for his body, clothes to ward off the chill and a dry place to sleep. That was enough for Jonas.

In a church shelter in North Carolina, a soft-voiced, sad-eyed woman gave him a winter coat. It was worn and the sleeves were too short, exposing his flat bony wrists and long broad hands. But it was made of good wool, and the pockets were deep and lined with flannel. And that was enough for Jonas.

The distinctive scent of spring sweetened the air by the time Jonas reached Virginia. The wind was chill, but the sunlight was bright with the promise of coming warmth. The now bushy beard he had let grow to protect his face from the cold began to itch. Jonas decided that the beard would have to go within a month or so.

He was tired. Having been unsuccessful in picking up a ride, he had walked the last twenty-five miles. Locating a shelter run by the Salvation Army, Jonas introduced himself as John, the name he'd used since that first time in Texas, and offered himself for work in exchange for food and rest for a few days. After receiving a dissecting stare from the army captain, his offer was accepted and, defying the clamoring inner urge, Jonas settled in to rebuild his stamina.

Jonas had been at the shelter five days and was feeling surprisingly good when, on glancing up from the bowl of soup before him, he had the strangest experience.

There was a woman seated at another long table nearby. Her back was turned, so he couldn't see her face, but there was something about her that riveted his attention. She was small and slender and had shiny black hair that fell to her shoulders. While he stared in fascination at her hair, Jonas was startled and shocked to feel a tightness in his chest; his breathing had become labored, too.

Stunned by the reaction of his body, Jonas sat and stared at the woman until she had finished eating and stood up. The minute she turned and he saw her face, the tightness in his chest began to ebb. Before she had crossed to the door to leave, his pulse rate had returned to normal. But moments later, Jonas felt a sharp pain sear through his head. Then it was gone. But not for long. Through the following two weeks, as Jonas slowly made his way to Baltimore, the pain struck with increasing persistence and severity.

Val looked forward to warm weather with both anticipation and dread. The winter had been hard and bitterly cold and she was eager to see new, lush green grass and flowers blooming in colorful profusion in her garden. But the warmer months would also bring with them anniversaries, so many anniversaries.

Val's birthday was in May. Their wedding anniversary and Jonas's birthday fell in June. Also in June was the anniversary of their reconciliation in San Francisco. Four weeks later it would be one year since Jonas had been kidnapped. And in August she would have to face the anniversary of the day she'd received notification of his . . .

No! Spinning away from the long dining-room window, Val headed for the stairs. She would not think about it. Blaming her wandering thoughts on her inactivity, Val quietly entered the nursery. Walking softly to the side of the crib, she gazed in adoration at the sleeping cause of her leave of absence from the office.

Lying on his belly, his face turned toward her, his small chin thrust out and his tiny hands curled into fists, Val's little Jonas was a youthful miniature of his father.

No, Val decided, she would not think of the horror, would not allow herself to dwell on the pain. Jonas had left her a precious gift in their son. She would not squander her time on useless remorse. She had a son to raise, a company to run and a family to care for.

Touching her fingertips to her lips, Val brushed her fingers over his silky black hair, the single feature of hers he had inherited, then turned and left the room.

She had things to do; she had to confer with Grace about the meal they would serve that coming Sunday, when Jonas's daughter and son-in-law and grand-daughter were coming for dinner.

The trucker stopped to pick up Jonas on I-95 outside Baltimore.

"Thanks for the lift," Jonas said, panting as he pulled himself up into the high cab.

"Sure," the trucker drawled. "Where ya headed?"

"North," Jonas answered.

"Well, I'm running to Allentown." The trucker grinned. "That far enough north for you?"

Jonas returned his grin and slumped against the seat. "That'll do. Thanks again."

Jonas had considered resting a while at a shelter on the southern edge of the city, but the sense of urgency was a constant now, eating at him, pounding through his bloodstream. The searing pain in his head was another constant, at times causing an instant of darkness, at others moments of brilliant shards of flashing lights. The pain was what had driven him to the highway. Now he was almost grateful for it.

"You can grab some sleep if you like," the trucker said, never taking his eyes from the roadway. "I won't mind. I'm not much of a gabber."

"I think I will," Jonas murmured on a sigh. "It's been a long haul." Somewhere in the neighborhood of six months, he added in weary silence.

Minutes after he shut his eyes, Jonas was deaf to the sound of grinding gears and the trucker cursing all Sunday drivers. Jonas dreamed of explosions and a dead man without a back, of hunger and thirst, of sweating as he trudged around a mountain and shivering as he walked along a backcountry road, and he dreamed of the back of a small, slender woman with shiny black hair.

The pain woke him. It was worse, intense, like knife blades stabbing into his skull. Jonas winced and sat up. He tried to read a road sign as the truck rumbled by it, but the lights were flashing inside his head and he couldn't focus.

"Where are we?" Jonas had to concentrate to articulate the question.

"Fifteen miles this side of Allentown," the trucker replied. "Give or take a mile."

Jonas felt sick. "If you don't mind pulling over, you could let me out here," he said between measured, pain-filled breaths.

"Makes no never-mind to me." Even as he spoke, the man sent the truck lumbering to the side of the highway.

"Thanks again," Jonas said, pushing the door open and jumping to the ground the instant the truck came to a halt.

"Sure. Have a good day."

The incongruity of the trucker's response didn't strike Jonas. He was beyond registering anything but the pain and flashing lights inside his head. Disoriented, he began to walk, but had taken less than a dozen stumbling steps when the inside of his head seemed to explode. The world turned a glaring red, then went black. Unconscious, Jonas pitched forward and into a shallow gully off the soft shoulder of the highway.

He was cold when he regained consciousness. The pain and the flashing lights were gone. He was clear-headed. Rolling to his feet, he stood and glanced around to get his bearings. A smile curving his thin lips, he started walking again . . . south. He knew exactly who he was and exactly where he was going.

Jonas Thorne was going home to his wife.

Without a twinge of doubt or hesitation, Jonas stepped boldly onto the highway to flag down the first police car to come cruising by.

"What's your problem, buddy?" the officer asked, running a wary glance over Jonas's rumpled appearance.

Briefly, concisely, impatiently, Jonas explained his situation. The officer was patently skeptical.

"Thorne?" His brow creased in thought, then his eyebrows flew into an arch. "What are you trying to pull, fella?" he demanded. "Thorne's dead. It was in all the papers."

Jonas bit out a brief curse. Since regaining consciousness, his imagination had been busy with speculation about the possible effects his disappearance had had, both on Val and everyone else. Val! Jonas groaned. Val thought he was dead! A new sense of urgency ripped through him.

Flicking Jonas a look of dismissal, the officer turned away. Jonas placed a hand on his arm, detaining him. "I am Jonas Thorne, officer," he said tersely. "And I can prove it. But first I've got to get home."

Something in his voice convinced the officer. Jonas got a ride home ... compliments of the Pennsylvania State Police.

Dusk shadowed the landscape when the police cruiser pulled into the driveway. Jonas's throat felt tight and his eyes smarted as he stared at the house. The windows were aglow with light. Only Jonas knew that the only light of any real value to him inside that house shone from the violet eyes of a small, dark-haired woman.

The officer loped behind Jonas as he strode to the front door. A frown touched Jonas's brow when he found the door unlocked. How many times had he cautioned Val about...? Jonas's thought splintered with the derisive laughter that lodged in his throat. Feeling suddenly light-headed, he turned the knob and pushed. The door noiselessly swung open on well-oiled hinges. Shaking and inexplicably scared, Jonas walked into the house. The sound of weeping drew him to the living-room archway. The scene that met his clouding vision was one of grief. Jonas absently noted the presence of his daughter and son-in-law, even that of the baby lying on a blue blanket on the floor. But his hungry gaze was riveted on the lovely, tear-streaked face of the small woman seated on the floor opposite his daughter, on the other side of the infant. Jonas felt odd, as if his head was floating. He had to work his throat several times before a sound emerged. And when it came, the droll sound of his voice amazed him.

"Is this a private wake, or can anybody cry along?"

The instant the words were out of his mouth, he knew he was losing it. But as the darkness closed in on his mind, he heard the sweetest sound imaginable, the sound that had fueled the inner urgency, driving him on for thousands of miles—the sound of Val calling his name.

"Jonas!"

Epilogue

Val sat by the bed in the quiet room, her eyes devouring the gaunt, hollow face of her husband. Jonas had slept through most of the nearly twenty-four hours that had passed since he'd fainted in the living-room archway. Except for checking periodically on the baby, who was in Grace's excellent care, Val had kept vigil by the bed throughout every one of those hours. She wasn't tired. Joyful energy hummed through her body, defeating weariness.

Her mind raced with images and impressions and Val knew that, should she live another hundred and thirty years, she would never forget a single detail of the scene in the living room and the hectic activity following it.

As they had seemed fated to do, Val and Mary Beth had once again been weeping over the uncanny resemblance of little Jonas to his father. Almost as if her unceasing grief had conjured it from the grave, the clear, dry sound of Jonas's voice had gone through Val like an electric shock.

Whipping her head around, Val had seen a wildly bearded, shabbily dressed specter standing in the archway. And though her intellect tried to deny it, Val had known at once who he was. Val was on her feet, running toward him before he hit the floor.

"Jonas!" Val's scream had shattered the sudden silence and the confusion in the minds of others. "My, God! Mary Beth, Jean-Paul, help me! It's Jonas!"

As she dropped to her knees beside Jonas, Val noticed another man stepping into the foyer. She was too distracted to see that he was uniformed. Before she could question his presence in her home, the man stepped forward to identify himself.

"Officer Switzer, ma'am, state police," he said respectfully. "Can you identify this man as Jonas Thorne?"

"What?" Val blinked, then nodded with distracted impatience. "Yes, yes, of course he's Jonas Thorne. I'm his wife." She moved her head to indicate the couple sinking to their knees on either side of her. "This is his daughter and son-in-law." While she spoke, Val's hands moved restlessly over Jonas, touching, searching, caressing his body, his face, his beard, his closed, sunken eyelids . . . *Jonas*.

The officer had proven to be of inestimable assistance. Not only did he volunteer to take care of the formalities by officially notifying the authorities about Jonas's return, he also helped Jean-Paul carry Jonas to the bedroom, undress him and get him into bed.

Val's right hand had made a more comprehensive examination of Jonas's face and body several times since then. She had rested her fingertips against his pulse, his steady beating pulse, at least a dozen times. Her left hand was enclosed within the steel-like grip of his right hand.

The first time Jonas awoke, Mary Beth broke away from Jean-Paul's supporting arm and flung herself onto the bed beside him, sobbing, "Daddy!" in a voice sounding like a young girl's.

"I'm here, honey. Don't cry. I'm all right. Everything's all right now."

Jonas's voice was calm, comforting. Only Val noticed the betraying tremor in his thin hands as he moved one restlessly over the girl's back, and the way the fingers of his other hand clenched in her hair, as if reassuring himself of his own reality by touching the flesh of his own flesh.

While holding his daughter close, Jonas's eyes, glittering with a frantic light, shifted searchingly. The frantic light only dimmed to a glow of satisfaction when his eyes settled on Val's soft violet gaze.

"Val." Jonas fell back to sleep with her whispered name on his lips.

It was late when Jonas woke again. Val was alone in the room. Promising to return in the morning, Mary

Beth had gone home to report the incredible news to Marge, Lynn and the company employees. The first words out of his mouth brought a smile to Val's soft, trembling lips.

"I'm filthy. I need a bath and a shave."

"You need food," Val corrected him.

His smile was tired, but it was there. "I'll make a deal with you," Jonas said, shoving back the bed covers. "You get the food while I get a bath and a shave."

"But Jonas!" she exclaimed anxiously. "Will you be all right on your own in there?"

His smile grew wry. "Sweetheart, I walked most of the way here from Central America," he drawled chidingly. "I think I can make it to the bathroom and back."

Val shuddered to even think of him walking that distance, then concentrated on getting together a light but nourishing meal for him, and worried about how he was doing in the bathroom.

As it turned out, Jonas did fine. He came out of the bathroom a few minutes after she returned to the bedroom. Her chest contracted at the sight of him, and she had to bite her lip to keep from crying out in concern.

His bones stood out in stark relief in his thin, hollow face and on his tall, angular frame. In fact, stark naked, he looked all bones, with skin stretched tautly over them. But his face was free of the bushy growth, and even drawn and gaunt, the face was definitely Jonas's.

He had barely wolfed down the meal before he fell asleep again, but before he did, he grasped her hand. Jonas had held on to her since then, his fingers tightly clasping hers even in slumber.

Grace had been in and out of the room countless times, bringing the baby to Val to nurse and supplying her with meals and coffee, fussing and generally checking on the condition of both of her employers. Earlier that morning, Val had asked Grace to call Jonas's family to inform them of his progress and to suggest that they wait to visit until tomorrow, since it was becoming obvious that Jonas needed as much sleep as he could get.

Now it was dusk again, and Val sat beside him, her hand in his, her eyes adoring his terribly gaunt, terribly drawn, terribly beautiful face.

As if he felt the loving warmth of her gaze, Jonas opened his eyes and stared directly into hers. His smile was beautiful. His voice was low, sexy, an open invitation.

"Why are you sitting there when there's so much empty space in this great big bed?" His hand tugged at hers.

Val blinked against a rush of happy tears. "I didn't want to disturb your sleep," she whispered.

"I'm not asleep now." His hand tugged again. "Disturb me."

Val didn't need to be coaxed. Slipping her hand from his, she stood and began walking around the foot of the bed, leaving a trail of discarded clothes in her wake. His warm gaze followed her every move. His hand groped for the edge of the covers, lifting them for her.

"Oh, Jonas. Oh, Jonas, you're home!" Crying openly now, Val slipped into the bed and into his crushing embrace.

"Yes," Jonas groaned, gliding his lips over her face and his hands over her trembling body. "Yes, I'm home," he repeated, crushing her mouth with his own.

"Jonas, wait!" Val cried out, laughing, when he released her mouth and moved his body over hers. "I have something exciting to tell you . . . show you!"

"It can wait," he growled against her mouth. "I can't. I remember, Val," he said starkly, settling into the silky cradle of her thighs. "Oh, God, I remember at last."

Val could hardly think for needing him, wanting him to be a part of her after so long. While her hands clasped his hips to draw him to her, she frowned and said, "Jonas, I don't understand. Why wouldn't you remember?"

Jonas laughed; it had the pure sound of joy. "It's a long story. I'll tell you all about it later. But right now—" his mouth brushed hers "—I need to kiss you, touch you, be absorbed by you."

Jonas and Val were one again, in unison, striving together for the ultimate perfection of ecstasy. When release sent them soaring, they joyously cried out each other's names.

"Jonas!"

"Val!"

Surprisingly, Jonas didn't go back to sleep. Exhausted, this time pleasantly so, he lay sprawled on his back and grinned at his wife.

"I want my present."

Val frowned. "What present?"

He arched a brow. "Didn't you say you had something exciting for me?"

Val's eyes flew wide. Then she laughed. She flew from the bed. Pulling on a robe, she dashed from the room, calling, "I'll be right back with your present. Don't you dare fall asleep."

When Val reentered the room a moment later, her arms cradling a sleeping infant, Jonas was yawning. His yawn melted into a soft smile as she approached the bed.

"My grandchild?" he asked softly, sitting up to get a look at the baby.

"No, Jonas," Val murmured, handing the sleeping child to him. He shot her a confused look. "Your son," she whispered. "Jonas Thorne, junior."

"My son?" His hoarse voice held awe and wonder. For long moments Jonas gazed down at the baby. When he looked up again, his eyes were wet and tears ran unheeded and unashamedly down his face. "Our son," he corrected her, almost choking.

"Yes, darling," Val whispered, slipping onto the bed beside him. "Our son."

Baby Jonas spent the remainder of that night sleeping peacefully in the big bed, between the protective bodies of his mother, Valerie, and his father, Jonas Thorne.

* * * * *

Coming in July from

Silhouette Desire

ODD MAN OUT #505
by Lass Small

Roberta Lambert is too busy with her job to notice that her new apartment-mate is a strong, desirable man. But Graham Rawlins has ways of getting her undivided attention....

Roberta is one of five fascinating Lambert sisters. She is as enticing as each one of her three sisters, whose stories you have already enjoyed or will want to read:

- Hillary in GOLDILOCKS AND THE BEHR (Desire #437)
- Tate in HIDE AND SEEK (Desire #453)
- Georgina in RED ROVER (Desire #491)

Watch for Book IV of Lass Small's terrific miniseries and read Fredricka's story in TAGGED (Desire #528) coming in October.

Silhouette Desire ®

1989
IS THE YEAR
OF THE MAN!

What makes a romance? A special man, of course, and Silhouette Desire celebrates that fact with *twelve* of them! From Mr. January to Mr. December, every month has a tribute to the Silhouette Desire hero—our **MAN OF THE MONTH!**

Sexy, macho, charming, irritating . . . irresistible! Nothing can stop these men from sweeping you away. Created by some of your favorite authors, each man is custom-made for pleasure—*reading* pleasure—so don't miss a single one.

Mr. July is Graham Rawlins in ODD MAN OUT by Lass Small
Mr. August is Jeremy Kincaid in MOUNTAIN MAN by Joyce Thies
Mr. September is Clement Cornelius Barto in BEGINNER'S LUCK by Dixie Browning
Mr. October is James Branigan in BRANIGAN'S TOUCH by Leslie Davis Guccione
Mr. November is Shiloh Butler in SHILOH'S PROMISE by BJ James
Mr. December is Tad Jackson in WILDERNESS CHILD by Ann Major

So get out there and find your man!

Silhouette Desire's

MAN OF THE MONTH . . .

MOM-1R